LIGHTNING STRIKES TWICE

' "*I don't suppose we shall ever meet again,*" '
she said the words aloud, quoting him. 'No I
don't suppose we ever will. He loved me while
he was with me, but not enough even to want
to keep in touch with me.'
It just didn't seem possible that life would go
on and that she must exist in a world that did
not hold him. It was impossible.
Suddenly she turned and went back to the
divan. She fell upon it burying her face in the
old brocaded cover, shivering violently. She
took Dominic's letter from her bag and held it
against her breast, crushing it.

Also by the same author,
and available in Coronet Books:

The Cyprus Love Affair
Forbidden
House Of The Seventh Cross
Gay Defeat
Do Not Go My Love
I Should Have Known
The Unlit Fire
Shatter The Sky
The Strong Heart
Stranger Than Fiction (Autobiography)
The Secret Hour
Nightingale's Song
It Wasn't Love
Fever Of Love
Climb To The Stars
Slave Woman
Second Best
Loving And Giving
Moment Of Love
Restless Heart
The Untrodden Snow
Betrayal (previously, Were I Thy Bride)
Twice Have I Loved

Lightning Strikes Twice

Denise Robins

CORONET BOOKS
Hodder and Stoughton

Copyright © 1966 by Denise Robins

First published in Great Britain by
Hodder and Stoughton 1966

Coronet edition 1968
Second impression 1969
Third impression 1976
Fourth impression 1977

Printed and bound in Great Britain for
Hodder and Stoughton Paperbacks, a
division of Hodder and Stoughton Ltd.,
Mill Road, Dunton Green, Sevenoaks,
Kent (Editorial Office: 47 Bedford Square,
London, WC1 3DP) by
Cox & Wyman Ltd., London, Reading and Fakenham

ISBN 0 340 02920 X

FOR

SHEILA VAN DAMM

I

ALL day it had been raining in Rome.

Cold, fine rain that changed to sleet. It was growing colder. Everybody thought there would be snow for Christmas which was only another two weeks ahead.

The young girl who was walking across the Bridge of Sant' Angelo shivered although she wore a warm, polo-necked jersey under her black, shiny mackintosh. A yellow silk scarf anchored her hair against the wind, but her face was soon drenched. She had to pull out a handkerchief and wipe her eyes as she walked quickly past the deep arched gate of the Orso.

It was then that the rain seemed to stop with miraculous speed and from the rift in the darkness of the sky there came a shaft of sunlight. Against this sudden translucent goldenness which was so much a feature of Rome, the frowning walls of the old castle looked wonderful. Magnificent, the girl thought and smiled. It was as though a storm within her heart had also passed and the world became suddenly brighter.

There were crowds on the bridge, and along the busy brightly lit thoroughfare as she passed down into the Via di Tordimona. The air was rich with the sonorous sound of the bells tolling the hour from the great churches.

It was the hour she loved. The hour that for so long now she had been able to call her own; to get away from the big palazzo where she had been living as an *au-pair* girl since June. When she could forget her two exacting little pupils, Francesca and Tullia. The hour when she could be herself, and go to *him*.

It was a never-failing joy to her—this afternoon walk to *his* studio. It had, in fact, become her whole life. She had learned that the emotions of a lifetime are easily piled into a few short moments. It had been like this ever since she met him. It seemed impossible now that she could ever have heard his

7

name with equanimity; that just before she first met him she had helped her pupils get into their party dresses and combed their shiny black curls, and prepared them to be sketched by the Duchessa's latest protégé—a young English painter whom they called Dominic—and felt indifferent when she heard the name.

The Duchessa had prattled a lot about the Englishman. She praised his genius as a portrait painter and seemed amazed that the English girl now living under her roof had never heard of him. The girl excused herself on the basis that she did not move in artist's circles in England, and knew little about pictures although she appreciated good art, and had learned much more about it since she came to Rome, with all its endless store of art treasures in museums and galleries.

She had also felt that she was justified in not knowing Dominic's name, because he had, apparently, been travelling for the last three years. His mother was Brazilian and his father English. He had been educated in England but later studied art in Paris.

He had money of his own and was by no means the struggling artist type; neither was he in any real need of the Duchessa's patronage. But she was a friend of his mother's and was a worldly, busy socialite—one of the leading hostesses in Rome who liked to produce 'lions' at her parties. Dominic was her latest lion. Dominic had agreed to do some quick sketches of her two daughters who were certainly beautiful little girls, with enormous eyes and that particular type of Italian beauty which the children lose quickly once they grow older.

The English girl hurrying through the damp and now sunny afternoon thought of her first meeting with the artist.

She could visualise him coming into the salon, portfolio under one arm; slight, not very tall, rather pale, but with an impressive head and bright challenging eyes. He looked, as the Duchessa said, as though he himself might be an Italian because of the darkness of his eyes, the olive of his skin and that mass of thick black waving hair.

It had been a warm September afternoon when he first came to the Del Farice Palazzo. He wore light blue linen slacks, a blue shirt open at the neck and had an old linen coat flung over his shoulders. There was nothing formal about Dominic. He had struck the English girl at once as being entirely indifferent to public opinion, absorbed in himself and his art. He cared for nothing and nobody—which was, of course, what made him different and so interesting.

He had interested her from the start. She sat without moving watching him draw the heads of the little Del Farice sisters. He worked with astonishing speed. He made an exact portrait of the two children and when he finished the frown that sat on his face while he worked changed into a sudden brilliant smile. He handed the work to the *au-pair* girl and said:

"There you are! Aren't they an angelic pair!"

She had looked down at the beautifully drawn heads and sighed deeply.

"How marvellous! You have made them look like two of Raphael's angels."

He had laughed.

"I'm no Raphael—I assure you."

"What are you?" she had asked.

"Just myself," he had answered rather haughtily. He had a supreme vanity which somehow took the wind out of one's sails. He fascinated her. He had fascinated her right from the start. What was more he behaved to her in a curiously insolent way which had made her at times angry, then amused, and finally gripped her imagination to such an extent that she could not think about anything or anybody but him. Nor could she do anything without wanting him to know about it.

He took entire control of her artistic education. She had re-visited the Sistine Chapel and seen all the wonderful art collections in Rome with Dominic as her guide and teacher. She had once thought she had a mind of her own. At home (the little ordinary English home that now seemed so many thousands of miles away) she used to be criticised because she refused to listen to other people or change any of her views. But for Dominic she changed most of them.

It had all started when he had asked her to go to his studio in the Via di Tordimona and allow him to paint her portrait.

She had gasped: "You can't want to paint *me*!"

"I wouldn't have asked you if I hadn't wanted it," he had snapped back.

He had looked quite angry. She had learned that Dominic could look very angry if his wishes were crossed. She had never met a man more spoiled—he was disgracefully egotistical. Yet whereas one might resent it in most men, one didn't resent it in Dominic. He was a law unto himself—different from anybody else and because he had so much charm when he chose to exert it—a positively devilish charm. Even the Duchessa who was married to one of the most handsome and wealthy titled men in Italy and supposed to be in love with her husband, had felt Dominic's magic. To the English girl, he had many wonderful qualities apart from his brilliance as a painter. He was moody, of course, but in the right mood he could be generous and kind. He also seemed to enjoy a certain reputation which he had of making love to the pretty women who sat for him. But the Duchessa had no intention of going as far as *that*, and she very soon got tired of lionising Dominic; so Dominic came no more to the Del Farice Palazzo. But the English girl went on seeing him.

To her absolute astonishment—and she hadn't yet got accustomed to it—he seemed to want to see her—a lot of her. She attracted him. He said so. He cut her short every time she tried to protest that she was ordinary.

"You are not, my dear. You're quite unusual. So small yet you have a natural dignity and aloofness which I find disarming. Glorious eyes too. Green as emeralds. One doesn't often see that shade of green. You have what I call a 'kitten face'. That flat little nose, your big mouth and those long-shaped eyes—very kitten-like, and endearing. But unlike kittens you don't scratch. You're gentle. You also have a damn good brain. I can talk to you and you understand and make intelligent conversation which is more than I can say of my girl-friends. All those beautiful spoiled girls in my mother's set out in Brazilia or here in Rome. Girls who are like your Duchessa—shallow, empty-headed and trying frantically to get one up over someone else all the time with their new clothes, new cars or new jewels. My little *au-pair* girl has nothing. Only her sweet self. I find it delightful."

He said many such things when she was with him. She alternated between being immensely flattered and rather cross—the latter because she felt there was a touch of patronage about his flattery. Yet she was staggered to find that she didn't want to stop him flattering her. For the first time in her life, and she was twenty-two, she had met a man with whom she could—and did—fall hopelessly in love.

'Hopeless' seemed the keynote to the whole affair. She knew that, but shut her mind to the future. He had warned her that he was not a marrying man (not that she ever imagined for a moment that Dominic would propose marriage to her). He had impressed it upon her that he was only a bird of passage in Italy and never stayed anywhere for long. He travelled from country to country, always able to enjoy the best that life could offer. He had plenty of money and need not rely on selling his pictures. Painting to him was a glorious hobby. He could paint when, where and who and what he wished; which was so much better, he told her than having to paint for a living. For then it became an inglorious profession—a prostitution of art—then one had to paint to please the public rather than one's self and one's soul.

Dominic talked a lot about his soul. He was interested in metaphysics, philosophy, all kinds of religions, almost anything but politics. He couldn't bear political discussions. He had little use for the minor problems, as he called them, of the average Englishman. Dominic had been born and brought up an Englishman. His father had once taken an active part in the political field, but Dominic was his mother's rather than his father's son—something of a dilettante. He had accepted an English education only because it had been forced upon him. He hated discipline in any shape or form.

He was the sort of person that seemed to the girl, who fell so completely under his spell, larger than life. A character out of a book. The type she had never expected to meet. Certainly not one she had expected to admire. But it was as though Dominic had put a potion into the first glass of wine she ever drank with him in that big luxurious studio of his at the top of a tall narrow house with great windows looking over the roof-tops across Rome.

She could not stop thinking about him—or longing for the next moment when she could see him. She would sit motionless while he painted or sketched her in a hundred different attitudes. She had become, so he told her, his favourite model. She soon grew used to seeing those paintings or sketches of her head and shoulders (and soon her whole body) in a dozen different poses.

Already one small painting of her in a scarlet woollen dress holding a black cat in her arms, had been bought by a well-known Italian director of a local art gallery. It had amused Dominic to make the green eyes of the cat and of the girl almost synonymous. When he had finished the work he had said to her:

"Actually those eyes of yours are extraordinarily incongruous. There's only a very small amount of 'cat' in yours, my darling. It's just the way you have of curling up and keeping warm and when you are happy I can almost hear you purr. But cats are sly and treacherous. You could never be either."

"But cats are very independent and I have always been accused of wanting to walk alone," she argued.

"I think the way our parents and friends at home see us differs entirely from the way we are regarded by the outside world," he had said.

Certainly that was true of herself. Since she first fell in love with Dominic, all her old spirit of independence seemed to have vanished. All that desire to be left alone or to enjoy introspection. Now she depended on another human being. Body and soul belonged to *him*.

This afternoon as she hurried towards his studio in the brief dying light of the December sun—she felt that same constriction of the heart—the same tightening in her throat—that she always experienced when she was on her way to Dominic.

How long would this continue? When would it all end? *It mustn't end.* In the beginning when he used to tell her that she must never fall in love with him, she had accepted it. She had assured him that she would conduct this affair in a practical modern spirit. Heaps of young people enjoyed intimate associations which were purely temporary. The 'love me for ever' theme was old-fashioned—outdated. Sensual love was wonderful while it lasted, but it was not deathless.

She had agreed with all these theories, and never let Dominic think her possessive. She knew quite well that other models came to his studio and that not only had there been other loves in his life but there were likely to be many more. If he preferred her company to the rest even for a little while, she should be grateful and content.

But she wasn't.

Her feelings suddenly underwent a change—a considerable change—a short time after she first fell in love with Dominic. Of course all her visits to Dominic's studio were secret. Her Italian employer knew nothing about them; nobody at home knew. She had never so much as mentioned Dominic's name either to her parents or her dearest friends. It was rather warm and exciting to have a secret love-affair. It made her feel in tune with her old ideas about independence. Why should she have to account to anybody for what she did? She was over-age. She had a right to a life and a love of her own.

But the secrecy and the excitement and the intense pleasure of loving and being loved by Dominic were gradually lost in a dark cloud of doubts and anxieties. She began to feel very unhappy. Panic tore at her every time she left him, wondering when she was going to see him again. She had learned that when walking to the studio she could feel like a person bewitched and float on magical wings—the wings of anticipation and desire. But when she walked away, she moved slowly and fearfully as though in a fog, crushed by a terrible sensation of insecurity that spoiled everything for her.

She could no longer feel happy in this love; no longer accept the fact that the day would come when it must all end.

Her terror of losing Dominic became a nightmare. She slept badly. She ate so little that she lost half a stone in weight and had to take in the bands of her skirts, and put up the hem of her dresses because they suddenly hung down far below her knees—she had grown so thin. Fortunately her mother was not there to take note of the change in her and the Duchessa was much too busy to notice whether the *au-pair* girl was thin or fat, rosy or pale. She was good with the children and taught them excellent English and that was all that mattered to the Duchessa.

Nobody, least of all Dominic, was aware of how the girl suffered. Even a man less egotistical than Dominic might find it difficult to realise what anguish such an affair could cause a woman. Men do not feel the same way about things; and this girl who until now had reached the age of twenty-two without having had her emotions stirred, suffered in particular.

The intensity of her own feelings frightened her. She did not *want* to love any man so much. It would have been all right if *he* had felt the same way, but she knew that he didn't. She was also frightened that he would guess and become irritated by her slavish devotion. So far she had managed to conceal it. He didn't like jealous and exacting women. He had told her so. So she showed neither jealousy nor the wish to pin him down. But she wanted with all her heart to chain him to her. She needed to know that he would never leave her—needed it until she reached the pitch of despair.

Why, why, she asked herself on this December day did she love Dominic so much? She knew all his faults. She was not so stupid as to be blinded by his immense charm, his fascinating personality—his talents. There were so many other qualities that she admired and which attracted her. His extraordinary generosity. For instance, he was surprisingly kind and thoughtful to those less fortunate than himself.

He filled his studio with impoverished artists—many of whom he financed. She knew that. She had met some of them. He was equally kind to the old and infirm. There was a caretaker in the block of flats where he rented his studio whose wife had been taken ill and died suddenly leaving the man with six small motherless children. It had been Dominic who paid for a splendid funeral because the family wanted it, with all the Italian love of ceremony and morbid interest in the trappings of burial. He supplied the man with enough money to engage a foster-mother, and sent the whole family into the country. He was always paying bills for the poor and there were many really poor people in Italy. The girl who saw this side of him loved him for it. Other rich men couldn't be bothered, but Dominic—so critical of the wealthy members of his own class and often so insolent and chilling to them—seemed to have boundless sympathy for the under-dog.

He had, the girl often told herself, a golden heart. Yet that goodness in him did not extend to the women in his life. She knew that, too. He frequently loved and rode away. He couldn't be bothered with his lovers once he grew tired of them. Then he became ruthless.

It was that knowledge that frightened her so much; the certainty that the day of reckoning must come for *her*.

For the moment it did not seem that the day was at hand because he seemed still to be deeply interested in her. Any time that she could get away from the Del Farice, she was invited to spend with him. They went out together constantly. They had been to every café or restaurant in Rome worth going to. He introduced her to the gay night-life as well as to Rome's intellectual delights. He had, in fact, educated her—mentally and physically.

There had even come a day—a night—when he had held her in his arms up in the warmth of his studio which she loved so much with its smell of paint and turps and all the trappings of Dominic's art—and told her that he really loved her.

"I really do," he had said. "There's something about you which has made you necessary to me and no other woman has ever been that before. 'Little Cat' . . ." (that was his pet name for her. *Little Cat*.)

When she heard what he said she felt as though her very heart leaped out of her body with joy. She began to feel a sudden hope that she need not be afraid of loving him. For the first time she was utterly, blissfully happy.

They had turned out the lights. They lay together on the big divan watching the leaping light of the log fire cast blue, freakish shadows on the high ceiling.

The curtains were drawn. Halfway down the wall through the enormous windows the girl could see the stars. The big cold stars that glittered so dramatically over Rome. She could hear the eternal tolling of the bells. Otherwise there was silence.

In a few moments she would have to let Dominic take her home. Yet this studio was really home to her—much, much more so than the Del Farice Palazzo; or the other home in England where she had been born and bred, never dreaming that she could ever experience anything as intense or wonderful as this love. It was a never-failing wonder and amazement to her that a man like Dominic should have become her lover.

Dominic was her life now. The very fact that until now she had believed in virginity and disliked the promiscuous affairs indulged in by so many of the girls and boys of her own generation bound her to him. To him it probably meant little or nothing. But to her it was of enormous importance and proof of how very much she loved him. That evening she was his as she had never been before. She was excruciatingly happy.

That had been a month ago. For her a wonderful period of time. Their hours together had never seemed more perfect and Dominic had never seemed more tender or more in love with her.

Then a fortnight ago, for the first time since their affair began, he broke their usual afternoon appointment. He had always been good about keeping appointments. He had never so far let her down. He could be cruel she was certain, but for some reason he had never been cruel to her. She had not as usual gone to the studio.

He had sent her a note by hand.

"Cara mia. Don't come today. I have to fly to Paris suddenly on business. Will let you know when I get back."

It was signed with the initial 'D'. It was the first and only note he had ever written her. She knew that he never wrote letters—particularly love-letters.

He did not communicate with her for ten days. It was terrible for her. Rome seemed dead and life utterly empty. The children irritated her and every time the telephone rang she hoped that it was for her—might be from *him*. But it was not. She kept wondering what kind of business had called him to Paris. She kept telling herself that it wasn't *her* affair what he did or where he went and that she had no right to probe into his private life, yet she had been so much part of that life for the last two months, how could she suddenly stand apart from it and behave as though he did not matter to her.

She suffered as she had never suffered before. She was appalled by her own capacity for experiencing such pain. It degraded her. She found it in no way uplifting.

She began to feel violent jealousy. She was petrified in case he never came back. Indignant because he behaved with such apparent indifference towards her. Furious because she felt he owed her more consideration, because of all that she had been to him. Then when she remembered how much less it must mean to *him*, she stopped being angry and just went down, down into the depths of misery again.

She made herself ill and finally retired to bed with a temperature which, the Duchessa said, was a touch of Roman fever.

Then suddenly Dominic telephoned to her from Paris and the whole world changed. It was still degrading in a way to have to realise what power he had to hurt—or delight her; what complete mastery he had over her. When she heard his voice over the wires her whole body burned.

"How are you, Little Cat?"

"Fine," she lied and laughed and was gay because that was what he liked.

"I shall be back in Rome on Saturday morning," he said. Mentally she counted. *Thursday, Friday, Saturday. Three more days* to go. Three days too long. But she laughed again.

"Terrific. I'll be round at the studio at four as usual."

"Of course," he said.

Then silence. Did she or did she not feel some constraint between them; or was it just that Dominic didn't want to say too much over the phone. Men were more cautious than women.

"Everybody's out," she said hopefully.

But he did not take advantage of this.

"See you on Saturday," he said. "*Au revoir*, Little Cat."

She started to speak again, but the line went dead.

For a long time she couldn't bring herself to return to the

salon where she had left the two children and continue their English lesson, her heart was beating too fast. She kept repeating to herself:

"*Thursday, Friday, Saturday*. Oh Dominic—*Dominic*!"

The next seventy-two hours seemed the longest of all. She was completely distracted, and even afraid that something might happen to detain him in Paris. How awful it would be if she got to the studio and didn't find him there! He might have an accident, but she would never know, or she might just hear about it casually, long afterwards, from the Duchessa who knew Dominic's mother.

The *au-pair* girl pictured her reunion with Dominic—a dozen times or more she pictured it and felt suffocated by the intensity of her feelings as she dwelt on the thought of their first embrace. His first long kiss on her hungry lips. He was such a marvellous lover. Or, of course, knowing Dominic, he might react quite differently and instead of embracing her, pick up a block and piece of charcoal, scowl at her and say:

"Don't move. Stay where you are. *Don't move*—that look on your face—I must try and capture it."

He had done this sort of thing several times in the past. She had had to curb her impatience to fly into his arms.

There came an awful moment when the Duchessa asked her to take the two children to their aunt on Saturday. She lived on the other side of Rome. The chauffeur would drive them there and bring them back for supper.

For the first time since she had come to the household, the *au-pair* girl rebelled and did not fall in with her employer's wishes.

"Oh *please*, if you could possibly do without me . . . I have made an important appointment . . . I rather want to keep it . . ." she stuttered and stammered, her cheeks fiery red.

The Duchessa seemed surprised and rather put out.

"Is it so important?"

Frantically, the *au-pair* girl thought up an excuse. A relative was arriving unexpectedly in Rome she said—just passing through—she had promised to go the airport and see her . . .

In the end the Duchessa relented and said that one of the

maids could take the children to their aunt. The *au-pair* girl breathed again.

Not to be able to go to the studio on Saturday and welcome *him* home would have been a disaster. She could not have borne it.

Now here she was taking the familiar route to the studio, feeling as though she was walking on air. She had been in love with Rome for a long time, but at this moment it seemed a city of such light and splendour that she was dazzled by it.

The Tiber flowed under the bridges like dark mottled gold. The outline of the Palatine and the Capitoline hills were darkly exquisite against the sky which was now heavenly blue. The clouds were gradually vanishing.

She wondered what Dominic would want to do this evening.

They would, of course, spend a few hours in the studio. Then perhaps he would take her to one of their favourite restaurants on the tiny *Piazza* of Sant' Ignazio where they would eat *fettucini*—Dominic's favourite *pasta*—with a carafe of red wine. And after the fruit and coffee, Dominic would probably pull out a block and start to sketch for the hundredth time, an antique fountain or a carved stone archway or some lovely little house behind wrought-iron gates, where there were ruined lichen-covered statues and moss-covered stone seats and an air of decay still beautiful in the sun, or this afternoon in the fading light which added to the air of romance and mystery.

Forever, the girl thought, Rome belonged to Dominic and to herself.

Oh Dominic, *Dominic!*

She came to the house in which he had rented his big studio from a young Florentine painter who had spent the late autumn here, and was now back in Florence.

She climbed the steep staircase, her high heels clattering on them and echoing. It was a long climb to the studio. There was no lift, but she didn't care.

Dominic—Dominic, she kept repeating his name softly to herself.

It was her custom to walk straight into his studio—he had

given her that right. He would be there waiting for her. He had said that he would be home this morning.

She would find him painting, or lying on the divan with his hands locked behind his dark, untidy head and a cigarette between his lips. When he got tired of work he liked to lie like that and, as he put it, contemplate. She could picture him—that slim body in the familiar, narrow slacks and polo-necked jersey—often black—which he wore for work. There was a certain restless grace and agility about him which at times reminded her of a ballet dancer. He was rarely still. His moments of 'contemplation' were brief.

Often she wondered what went on in his mind. Often when she was physically close to him she felt mentally far apart, and as though she lay in the arms of a stranger. Often she had felt that it was foolish and futile to love Dominic too much or try to get too close to him. But this afternoon she rushed into the studio full of anticipation—eager—radiant.

She stopped dead on the threshold. One quick glance around the big high-ceilinged room told her that Dominic was not there. But the caretaker whose family Dominic had befriended was on his knees, washing the floor. For one horrified moment, she stared down at him. He greeted her in Italian, smiling, then rose to his feet and wrung the water from his floor-cloth into a bucket.

"Where is the *Signor*, Antonio?" she demanded.

He shrugged his shoulders. He did not know, he said, but he pulled a letter out of his pocket.

"For you, *Signorina*."

She was no stranger to Antonio. He accepted the fact that she was always here, and was the English *Signor*'s very special model.

She took the letter gingerly as though it burnt her fingers.

"How did this come?" she asked, thankful that she could speak the man's language. "Who gave it to you?"

"The *Signor*, himself."

"He has been here?"

"Yesterday he came, *Signorina*, but he packed and left in a hurry."

A wave of nausea passed over her. She went cold—ice-cold.

She began to breathe fast. She stared at the caretaker a little crazily.

"What do you mean, Antonio, he left in a hurry?"

The Italian looked unhappy. He was, like all Italians, in love with love and did not like to see the beautiful English *signorina* look so upset. Shrugging, he waved a hand around the studio. She saw its emptiness. It was painfully clean, too. Antonio had almost finished washing and dusting. All the pictures had gone from the walls. The many portraits that he had painted of her as well as of other girls. It hit her hard. A knockout blow—seeing this emptiness and order, those blank walls on which there were marks of discoloration, showing where the pictures once used to hang.

The caretaker with unusual delicacy of feeling picked up his bucket and started to walk out of the studio thinking that the *signorina* might want to be alone. She let him go, but called him back.

"What time did the *Signor* come here? When did he leave again?"

"He came about midday," Antonio said. "He left just before half past one in a big car with a chauffeur; possibly a hired one, *Signorina*, I do not know, but I helped carry the luggage into the car and I heard the *Signor* say to the driver: 'Back to the airport now.'"

It seemed that the *Signor* was catching a plane. Further than that he could not say.

He went out and shut the door.

The girl went on standing still for a moment clutching her letter. She was afraid to open it although she told herself that it was quite obviously a letter of 'good-bye'. A good-bye that Dominic had not had the courage to say in person.

The terrible suddenness of the break and the extreme bitterness of her disappointment, after being so happy, crushed her. She found it painful to breathe. How she had run up those steep stairs! Dear God, up as though to the stars! Dear, *dear* God, what an anticlimax! This cold empty studio—all that the coldness and emptiness *meant*.

She forced herself to walk to the divan and sat down. She dared not read her letter, yet she must. She must see what he had to say to her, what excuse he had to offer for doing this dreadful, cowardly thing?

Only three days ago he had spoken to her on the telephone and told her that he would come back this morning and that he would see her this afternoon at the usual time. What could possibly have happened during those three days to make him change his mind and return only to pack and go away again without seeing her? She felt that this must be one of her nightmares and that she would soon wake up and see him come through the door as he had done dozens of times with a long loaf of bread under one arm, and a bottle of wine, and one of the small black cigars that he enjoyed smoking, between his lips. He would put the bread and the wine on the table and say:

"Here's the saucer of cream for my Little Cat."

She looked down at the envelope. He had written her full name. It looked frighteningly formal to her. Dominic had a large rather untidy writing for a man. She grit her teeth and tore open the envelope. She felt she would be incapable of taking in the words unless she said them aloud so she began to recite the letter. It was untidy with several words crossed out, but that was typical of Dominic. He was an untidy person.

"My dear—" it began, "I don't quite know what to say to you. I feel all kinds of a rat for walking out on you. I didn't mean it to happen this way. That, I swear. I know I warned you that marriage is not for me, but I also admit that with you I outran the usual distance of any love-affair I have ever had. I told you I loved you. That was right, but also wrong. I can't really love anybody completely. I am not capable of it. That's my loss, but we are what we are and few can change. You, on the other hand, love too much. You sink the ship with so many gifts, my darling. You gave me far too much. I am grateful, but I couldn't give back as much.

I really did mean to go on seeing you and being happy with you and, I hope, making you happy, until your job in Rome ended as you said it would do this summer. But what happened in Paris changed everything. My mother arrived—it was because of her that I originally went over. As you know, my father died when I was young and my mother married again—a Brazilian younger than herself whom I very much disliked so for a long time I haven't seen much of Mama. The husband was killed in a car smash a short while ago since when she has been ill and unhappy. I am very fond of her and would have stayed with her if I hadn't thought that she would probably marry again because she's still barely fifty and very beautiful. But she has cancer and only four or five months to live. She came to Paris to see a specialist in whom she had great faith, but he could do nothing. I was appalled to see her looking so thin and sick, and half drugged. There was a nurse with her. I promised to go back to Brazil and stay with her until she doesn't need me any more.

So the parting of the ways has come for us, my dear, and I don't suppose we shall ever meet again. I acknowledge my cowardice, but I just couldn't face you, Little Cat. You are somehow too vulnerable. I thought a scene would tear us both in pieces so I've run away from it. I couldn't even warn you on the telephone. I'm a selfish brute, but not brutal enough perhaps. I really did mean to see you right up to the end and that is why I didn't write to the Palazzo. I knew you would come to the studio.

Try to forgive me. At least I'm not in love with anybody else—I promise you that—nor likely to be. You were very generous and sweet to me. I thank you, and in my fashion I loved you.

Don't be unhappy. I should hate that.

Dominic"

Slowly the girl folded the letter, put it back into the envelope and dropped it into her bag. It took some time before the whole significance of it reached her and then, much as she had loved the man, she could not fail to see the appalling egotism in every line. He had *known* she would go to the studio. Yes, of course, but he couldn't face her. Oh God, what a thing to do.

The first terrible pain of finding Dominic gone was passing. Now she was gripped by a sickness of heart and mind and a despair worse than physical pain.

One line in the letter stood out.

"At least I'm not in love with anybody else."

She almost laughed. Was that supposed to help? Would she have felt any worse if there had been another girl in Paris —or Brazil—or anywhere? Perhaps! Perhaps it made things a little easier to know he had only gone because his poor mother was so ill. And of course it was in keeping with that *kindly* streak in Dominic which made him sensitive to the pain of others that he was taking her home. He realised that *she* who loved him was 'vulnerable'. He had said so in the letter. So sensitive was he in fact that he hadn't been able to face her. He had left her to endure this ghastly shock quite alone. She couldn't get over the agony of that mistake on his part.

"'*I don't suppose we shall ever meet again,*'" she said the words aloud, quoting him. "No I don't suppose we ever will. He loved me while he was with me, but not enough even to want to keep in touch with me."

It just didn't seem possible that life would go *on* and that she must exist in a world that did not hold him. It was *im*possible.

Suddenly she turned and went back to the divan. She fell upon it burying her face in the old brocaded cover, shivering violently. She took Dominic's letter from her bag and held it against her breast, crushing it.

2

CRESSIDA pulled the rose and cream floral silk dress and short jacket out of its tissue paper wrappings in the big box, put it on a hanger and hung it up outside the door of the built in cupboard in her bedroom. For a moment she looked at it with pride and satisfaction.

"My going away dress . . ." she said the words aloud "Going, going away! . . . Right away from the old life to the new. Pink dress—I wonder if you realise how important you are!"

She turned and looked around her, grimacing. The room was in complete disorder, several open boxes; two new airways suitcases, odd garments spread over carpet, chairs and bed. What a mess, she thought. This was a time when she wished that there had been a spare room in which she could spread herself. But there was only one spare and that was used by Daddy. Poor Daddy!

Dr. Raye, retired, victim of polio that had kept him in an iron lung for a year and a wheelchair for the last six years, used the room that had been intended for guests. It was his study and, as he called it, bolt-hole. He needed a lot of peace and quiet these days, and there wasn't much of either in the big sitting room and dining room combined where the rest of the family gathered. Cressida had never been the noisy kind, but her brother Simon, aged fourteen still at public school seemed in the holidays to turn the whole place into a background for pop music, and the antics and games of his boisterous friends.

It hadn't been an easy life for poor Mummy, Cressida thought this afternoon as she tried to bring a little more law and order into her particular room. Fortunately, Daddy had had private means, but it had been a struggle to run the home once Daddy was no longer able to practise. There had been Cressida's own school fees, her brother's to follow and the upkeep even of this small place stretched the family resources to the uttermost. Mummy did all the cooking as well as looking after her invalid husband with only the help of a daily.

A year after John Raye fell ill they had had to sell their big attractive Sussex house in Hurstpierpoint, and buy this bungalow in Brighton. The whole family disliked Brighton—and bungalows. But it had seemed at the time the one thing for a man who had to spend the rest of his life in a wheelchair.

It had worked. It was a well-built bungalow, with a good garden of about half an acre and a view of the Downs.

Freda Raye with her genius for homemaking and her love of colour and design had been clever with the décor. She had made it all look attractive. She was Austrian by birth but after twenty-five years in England had become thoroughly Anglicised and spoke English with only the faintest trace of an accent.

She came into Cressida's bedroom now, waving a small hatbox.

"*The* hat, poppet! Let's see it on you."

She threw the little box at Cressida who caught it laughing.

"You've seen it on already, Mum."

Freda Raye forgot the hat and walked up to the rose pink two-piece, fingering it, uttering little cries of admiration.

"Oh! Oh! So *that's* come too! What excitement, my darling."

Cressida sighed, cleared a place for herself on the untidy bed and reached for a packet of cigarettes. As she lit one she looked with a strange feeling of sadness at her mother.

How come, she wondered not for the first time, had she ever managed to be born of anybody so different from herself? Mrs. Raye was a big, full bosomed, fair haired woman—a whole head taller than Cressida; still handsome at forty-nine, although she had let her figure go and generally wore either slacks while she was working—they didn't suit her because her hips were too broad—or a tweed skirt with a jersey which had shrunk after too much washing or cleaning. Not a glamorous figure, but as Cressida knew well, her mother could still look quite beautiful when she took a little trouble and put on

26

a nice dress. She had kept her lovely pink and white complexion and there was only a touch of grey in the gold hair which she wore plaited round her head. She had rejected all other hair styles.

Her cooking was famous in her circle of friends. She worked hard and never spared herself. She still worshipped the man she had married when he was a young, good-looking attractive man. All their friends admired Freda Raye. It seemed such a pity to Cressida that she had never felt close to her mother; never been able to confide in her, nor respond often to the somewhat exuberant love that Mrs. Raye offered to both her children. Great hugs and smacking kisses. '*Darlings*' continually rolling off her tongue. Nothing too much trouble for either of them. She spoiled them, but it was Simon, her fair blue-eyed son, so like her, whom she completely understood and who adored her. Cressida was like her father—a much more remote, unapproachable character.

Cressida found it difficult to show her feelings. She rather shrank from anybody who made an effort to get too close to her. She knew that she was a disappointment to her mother who, when Cressida was a child, used rather stupidly to complain that "Cress didn't love Mummy". Cressida could remember on one occasion when her father had taken her on one side and said:

"Be good and kind to your mother, Cress. She has a warm, generous nature. She's one of the 'givers' in this life. In fact she gives too much. It's up to us to try and repay her."

Cressida used once to feel, guiltily, that she had never sufficiently repaid Mummy. She couldn't help it. Devouring maternal love somehow smothered her.

Both Cressida's parents were delighted that she had found Sam. He who was not only a terribly nice person, but had a good job. He had recently become a junior partner with his uncle's firm of stockbrokers. He seemed heart and soul in love with Cressida.

This morning Cressida's mother felt full of pride and joy as she looked at her daughter.

"Can I pinch one of your cigarettes, darling?" she asked in her warm rich voice. "About everything we ordered has

27

come now," she added. "When are you going to start packing, at least one case? I wish you'd let me—"

"No, thanks, Mummy," cut in Cressida hurriedly. "I'd like to do my own packing."

Mrs. Raye, disappointed, as usual, by her daughter's lack of co-operation, smiled bravely.

"I'm so good at it."

Cressida relented. She touched her mother's arm.

"You're so good to me. You can pack if you want."

"No, no, not if you don't want me to, darling."

There followed one of those little arguments which Cressida always dreaded and which her mother, having won her way flung the honours back at her and so it went on until one of them gave way. Today's argument ended in Cressida's defeat because she felt that she was never nice enough to poor Mummy.

"You're jolly well *going* to pack for me now. I'll leave everything just as it is, all over the place, and between now and Saturday—you can do it all. Serve you right," she said gaily.

Mrs. Raye beamed.

"Is Sam coming down tonight?"

"Yes, he's taking me out to dinner. I told you so this morning, Mummy."

"Sorry, darling, I forgot."

Now Freda sat down beside her daughter and put an arm around her. Feeling noble, Cressida did not edge away from all that warm affectionate flesh that yearned towards her. She even nuzzled her mother's shoulder with her cheek.

"Dear old Mum! This wedding means a lot to you, doesn't it?"

"Of course. All mothers enjoy such things. It's going to be a great day and you will make such a beautiful bride. You are such a beautiful girl, my darling. Everyone says so. So unusual."

"Very unusual," said Cressida with her tongue in her cheek.

"Sam adores you."

"I love Sam."

"Ah! How I like to hear you say that. It means the gr-r-

28

reatest happiness for you both because you love each other so much," exclaimed Mrs. Raye who only rolled her r's when she was really excited or moved. "I never thought this time would come, although your father told me it would. He was like you when he was young Cressy—so difficult to please. There were no girls in his life until he went to that Medical Conference in Vienna and met me . . ." Freda's big, heavily lidded blue eyes grew soft and reminiscent, "and then he was *so* much in love. Such a wonderful lover. You will be the same."

Suddenly Cressida could no longer bear her mother's enveloping warmth or the tender sentimentality that spilled from her. She got up and put the going-away dress into a cupboard.

"So that you don't pack this by mistake, Mum," she said rather abruptly.

Mrs. Raye put her cigarette between her lips and looked around her. This bedroom was the only one Freda had not attempted to decorate when they moved into the bungalow. Cressida had been seventeen then and had strong ideas of her own about décor. They differed from her mother's as everything else differed with them. Freda liked floral designs, sugar-pinks, baby blues, gilded angels and crystals from Vienna. Cressida's nature was depicted in this room. Rather Swedish in design, austere, modern, with tobacco-brown carpet, white walls, and curtains that had a pattern of wild looking ponies with flowing tails and manes. The furniture was greyish wood. The lamp by the bed had an enormously tall, white, narrow shade. There were shelves of books—the sort that Freda would never read—such as Leonardo da Vinci's *Notebook*, Jean-Paul Sartre, Iris Murdoch; a catholic taste. There were two framed photographs on the dressing table, one of Simon, one of her parents taken together years ago, and over the mantelpiece a lovely coloured reproduction of Adam's head and shoulders, a detail from the Michaelangelo ceiling in the Sistine Chapel. Cressida knew a lot about painting, but since her return from Rome she seemed to have lost interest in it.

To the mother, her daughter was too deep, too remote for

understanding. Dr. Raye continually assured his wife that under Cressida's deep, dark surface there burned a fire. Freda tried to believe that it was so and to console herself with thoughts of Wagner opera to which *she* was addicted—the belief that a lover's kiss would one day awaken this small sleeping Brunhilda.

How beautiful Cressida was, Freda thought fondly this morning. *Petite*, with a tiny waist, and small softly swelling breasts. She had her father's straight, dark hair. It curved across one cheek. She wore it rather long. The almond-shaped eyes were a strange light green under thick black lashes, and her brows slanted upward. Her mouth was rouged pale pink, rather sad in repose, but the sadness vanished suddenly when she smiled.

The Rayes had been glad when a year ago their daughter accepted a job in Italy as an *au-pair* girl teaching English to the small daughters of the Duchessa Del Farice. A mutual friend living in Rome had made the initial introduction. They encouraged Cressida to go to Rome. She had been so much at home helping with the domestic chores, and the invalid after she left school. In fact, she hadn't taken a job before because she had felt it her duty to help her mother, especially when her young brother was home for the holidays. Dr. Raye could do absolutely nothing for himself and Freda couldn't do the heavy lifting alone. But when the Italian opportunity came, they had insisted on Cressida leaving them. The District Nurse could come in and help Freda and they agreed that the girl needed a complete change of environment.

At first she had written quite happily—although she was not a prolific correspondent. But she seemed to get on very well. She had always been deeply interested in art and she found Rome fascinating. Then her letters grew less frequent, and more non-committal. It was a surprise to the Rayes when she suddenly arrived home for Christmas. She had meant to stay in Italy a whole year. Freda, never one to probe deeply, accepted Cressida's explanation that she had just 'had enough' of Rome and wanted to be home again. She found it rather touching that Cressida should want to return and help her. Dr. Raye thought his daughter had changed and grown nervous and restless. Something, he thought, seemed to be preying on her mind.

Freda disagreed:

"I think if she *has* changed it's for the best," was her comment. "She has come out of her shell a lot. I'm glad of it. She goes out more. She doesn't mope around reading and dreaming like she used to do."

Dr. Raye did not press his point, but in his opinion, Cressida had started to be rather *too* gay and to laugh a little too loudly. She had even turned her back on art and classical music and joined young Simon in his quest for Pop Groups and the latest dance records. Dr. Raye worried. But Freda didn't, and was delighted when Sam Paull suddenly appeared on the scene and the one thing that Freda had always prayed for happened.

Cressida met the Right Man and he fell in love with her.

On this bright summer morning in July, Freda began to clear up a few of the boxes and the masses of tissue paper that were lying around Cressida's bedroom and dreamed happily about the forthcoming wedding day.

The telephone bell was ringing as Cressida walked into the hall. It ran the length of the north side of the bungalow. All the rooms faced south. The door of the big double sitting room was open. The brightness of the July sunlight streamed through the long picture window. Cressida could see what a lovely day it was—green and amber shadows dappling the swelling breasts of the Downs. After five years the garden was beginning to mature; the multicoloured roses in the round beds were beautiful. There was one lovely cherry tree which was Dr. Raye's pride and joy, and half a dozen standard roses in a semicircle around an old stone bird bath which had come from their former home. The lawn was green and fresh. A macrocarpa hedge separated the flower garden from a little patch in which they grew a few vegetables. Cressida's mother was quite good with gardens and with her unbounding vitality managed to work in it when she wasn't at the kitchen sink. John Raye, dauntless and determined not to become an entirely useless cripple, liked to wheel himself up and down, weeding the beds with a long implement which a local ironmonger had made especially for him.

The air was always fresh up here. It was so fine and clear this morning that Cressida could see a rim of blue green sea far below the hill and across the house-tops of Brighton. But to her the bungalow had never really been home like the old house of her childhood. She liked period places.

Just for an instant nostalgia seized her heart as she stood thinking, and remembered Rome. The great columns, the carved stone arches, the glorious fountains sparkling in the sun.

But it was a fleeting memory. She never really permitted herself to think about Rome. Being strong minded, she had tutored herself not to do so. It was as though she had lived two lives. One was dead. *That* love was dead. It had died in a studio at the top of an old house in the Via di Tordimona. From that day to this she had never heard from *him* and fiercely she had erased the very name of Dominic from her mental register. Today she lived another, different life. She was quite a different person.

The telephone rang again. She answered it. As she heard the voice of the man she was so soon to marry, she felt less tense. She spoke to Sam happily and in the teasing way which he seemed to enjoy.

"I thought you were supposed to be hard at work, Mr. Paull. No work means no money. No money, no wedding. I've already told you I'm only marrying you for your fortune."

Sam's rather deep throaty laugh answered her.

"Then you've backed the wrong horse, my love. I haven't a shilling to bless myself with."

"Not even a *shilling*?"

"No—not sixpence."

"Then I'll post back your ring. No—I'll give it to you in person tonight, to save the stamp."

"Darling," said Sam on a warmer, lower note, "I'm terribly in love with you, you know."

"You're sweet, Sam—much too sweet to me."

"I could never be sweet enough to you. You're such a special person."

"What's so special about me?" She tried to tease again.

"I haven't time to tell you why you're special just now. But I'd like to remind you that in a few days you will be my wife. Mrs. Richard Samuel Paull, remember?"

She repeated the name and added:

"It sounds fine. Is this really why you've rung me? What can they think in the office?"

"It's empty. Tea break. They are all busy drinking their cuppas. Uncle Richard is on the Floor. I've just come back from seeing a chap on business in Mincing Lane and I've got the office to myself."

"What's the market like this morning?"

"You do amuse me, my darling, when you try to show an interest in stockbroking."

"Oh, but I *am* interested, Sam. After all I'm going to be a stockbroker's wife. I must know something about you being either Bullish or Bearish."

"Darling, I do love you," he roared with laughter now. "You're *terrific*! And if you want to know, everything is pretty 'bearish' just now. What with the confused situation of our internal politics, Viet Nam, and the rest of the troubles abroad, nothing's moving on the Stock Market. Uncle Richard was saying only this morning that we would all be on the rocks if it wasn't for our nice big Unit Trusts and New Issues. They keep our heads above water." Then suddenly in a changed voice, he added: "Thank you very much for letting me know."

"Letting you know what?" she began mystified.

"Good-bye, now," said Sam, clearing his throat.

Cressida's eyes danced as she put down the telephone. She understood. Uncle Richard had probably walked back into the office. He was a humourless type who wouldn't approve of the junior partner 'palavering' with his fiancée right in the middle of a morning's work. The routine of Messrs. Paull, Leafe & Paull must continue its mercenary course, uninterrupted.

3

CRESSIDA stood still a moment twiddling her diamond and ruby engagement ring around her finger. At times it seemed impossible to her to believe that there would soon be a narrow gold circlet on that finger as well. That this time next week she, as Mrs. R. S. Paull, would be in Majorca on her honeymoon. And then she would be returning to live in her own home in the village of Cowfold.

Cowfold was not more than twelve miles from Brighton so she would find it easy to see a lot of her parents. When Sam had asked her which part of the country she wanted to live in, she had said not too far from home because poor Daddy adored her so, and because her brother, Simon, was still so young and in the holidays Sam would make such a very good stand-in for Daddy. In a wheelchair, Daddy could do little for a schoolboy son.

Simon loved sport. Sam was just the right brother-in-law for him. Sam was a Rugby football enthusiast who never missed an International Match at Twickenham unless he could help it. Already, to young Simon, he was a sort of god. So, when Cressida and Sam agreed that they neither of them wished to live in London and Sam was willing to 'commute'— they settled on Cowfold in Sussex. They had found an enchanting Regency cottage near the village. Just the sort of square, white little house Cressida had always longed for. A fat cheque from Uncle Richard, who was a rich man, had helped tremendously towards the initial payment and the decorating and furnishing. And if they couldn't yet afford all the modern luxuries such as central heating, they would come in time. Cressida and Sam agreed that it was better to start life with a really nice place and nice things even if it meant being a bit uncomfortable.

They were in agreement over a number of other things such as love of the country, gardens and antiques. Sam—

unusual for a young man of his type—liked to potter around the antique shops and was knowledgeable about period stuff. He and Cressida also shared a liking for good food, winter sports, and dancing.

Cressida, partial to beauty in any shape or form, admired Sam Paull from the very first moment she saw him. It struck her that the Ancient Greeks would have chosen him as a sort of sun-god. He was such a radiant person. His thick, fair hair was touched with gold, like his lashes. His eyes were brilliant blue and his pinkish skin glowed with health, like his strong white teeth. When Cressida first met him, he had just returned from a ski-holiday in Switzerland. His tan had made him more than usually attractive. He had nice hands, too, which was something Cressida appreciated in the opposite sex.

She remembered when she had first been introduced to him at a party given by an old school friend who was, herself, married to a Stockbroker. Betty Chalmers had led Cressida across the room to Sam, whispering:

"I know you'll say he's too good-looking but he has none of the usual drawbacks of handsome men. He isn't conceited or effeminate. He's a hundred per cent masculine. He isn't promiscuous, either. Geoffrey knows him pretty well and says he gets all the women running after him without trying, but he's really rather scared of them and keeps most of them well at arm's length. He isn't one of the ones that wants to pop in and out of bed all the time—I'm quoting Geoff, of course!"

Now Cressida had no need to take any notice of what Geoffrey Chalmers or anybody else thought about Sam Paull. She had learned all about Sam for herself. He had fallen in love with her at first sight, but he had certainly never tried to 'pop into bed' with her. He was rather old-fashioned in his attitude towards girls and made no exception in her case.

"If there's no respect, I don't see how there can be love—real love," he had said during one of their long discussions when they got to know each other better.

It sometimes struck her that poor Sam didn't really know her at all well and that all the odds were on her side. But he seemed content. Sometimes she wondered uneasily if he would feel that same respect and regard for her if he knew about the *other man*. Several times she had been on the verge of telling him. He was neither a prig nor a prude. Hundreds of men married girls in these days knowing that they had had serious love affairs before. But somehow she hadn't been able to bring herself to tell him about Dominic or even mention his name. She argued with herself that it was *her* affair and *her* life; not Sam's. What had happened was in the past. The present and the future belonged to Sam. She meant to be a good wife to him.

She had turned down his first few proposals of marriage. She did not want to love or be loved by Sam. He wasn't really her kind. He was the complete antithesis of Dominic. Besides, whatever she felt, it would, she decided, be unfair to Sam to marry him.

But the big, fair, handsome young man went on bombarding her with love ... with his flowers, his letters, his telephone calls. He took her to the theatre, to dinner, to dance. She had only to mention some small thing that she wanted and it was there for her the next day. He was generosity itself and most attentive. There was nothing of the egotist about Sam.

She began to change her mind. Sam was just Sam. He had nothing in him that could remind her of Dominic. Nor did their companionship bear any resemblance. With Dominic it had been *she* who gave everything. Now it was her turn to be worshipped. It was almost a relief to be able to feel that her lover loved her more than she loved him.

With the brightness of Sam's wings folded so closely about her she was able to relax. To start giving him as complete a devotion as he gave her. It seemed a long time ago now—yet it was barely a month since they became engaged.

On that particular June night, he took her to dine in Hampstead with his mother who had recently married again— The second husband was Sir Guy Fennell, Bart. It was in his big Victorian house facing Hampstead Heath that they were now living. A small self-contained flat had been made on the top floor for Sam.

A few weeks previously at Cressida's first meeting with Sam's mother, she had not really liked her much. Lady Fennell was the type Cressida would call 'tricky'. On the surface, she was sweet enough, but rather too sweet, too gushing to be genuine. She was still very pretty for her forty-seven years and as *petite* as Cressida. It seemed that Sam had inherited his height from his father although his colouring was his mother's.

But one thing Cressida soon learned was that Sam was nothing like his mother in character. The late Martin Paull had been a charming man of absolute integrity. Sam was similar. But Frances Paull, known in her intimate circle as 'Franny', could be difficult and even unpleasant. A sting lay under the sweetness and, when it suited her she used it.

It soon became apparent to Cressida that Lady Fennell had lined up another girl for her son and was not pleased when Sam took Cressida home. This other girl, Diana Marshall, was an heiress and came from a Leicestershire hunting family. Franny took pains to discuss Diana—linking her name with Sam's—at the very first dinner party she gave for Cressida (at her son's request).

Cressida had been admiring the beautiful house, full of glorious old furniture and paintings. She did not usually move in quite such a high stratum of society. She thought it all very elegant, but she was glad that Sam was more simple in his tastes, and so unassuming. It was quite a shock to Cressida to find that the only thing that really mattered to pretty Lady Fennell was money. She had married old Sir Guy for his money-bags alone. He was twenty years older than she was. Cressida found Sir Guy a nice friendly old man, far too easily and too often bullied and badgered by his extravagant selfish wife. But he still adored her and paid her bills. Her main recreation was gambling—on the race course or in the casinos of Europe.

Cressida admired Franny's good looks, her lovely clothes, her poise. She was so much a woman of the world—so different from poor old untidy Mummy, mooching around the kitchen in an overall with a cigarette between her lips. But Cressida preferred Mummy and she soon learned to feel contempt rather than admiration for Sam's mother. She felt sorry for Sam, too. He was loyalty itself and never said one word against his mother who even made him call her 'Franny' instead of 'Mother' because she did not want her age to be broadcast. Cressida felt that she must be a disappointment to her affectionate, big-hearted son.

The bitch in Franny first showed itself when at dinner she called Cressida by some other girl's name, then with a tinkling laugh corrected herself:

"Sorry, darling. My sweet Sam has so many girl friends I never can remember all their Christian names, although I must say he sees more of dearest *Diana* than most of them. You must meet Diana some time."

Cressida looked across the dinner table at Sam. His usually gay blue eyes were angry.

"That's rather misleading, Franny!" he said quietly. "I don't, as you know, have a lot of girl friends."

"But *Diana*, dear—" began Franny with a sly look at Cressida.

"Let's talk about something else," said Sam quite sharply.

Afterwards when he was sitting next to Cressida, smoking the cigar which his stepfather had given him, he made haste to tell her that Franny 'liked to exaggerate'.

Cressida, well aware of what was going on, and right on Sam's side, assured him that she understood. But she could not resist teasing him.

"*Is* Diana *the* girl in your life?"

"No, *you* are," he whispered and took her hand and pressed it ardently.

She decided to ignore Lady Fennell's malice.

On the way home Cressida announced to Sam that she was quite sure his mother didn't like her.

"Not true—she is just *Franny*," Sam apologised for his mother. "At the moment she has got it into her head that she wants me to marry Diana, but I have no intention of doing so, I assure you, *and* she knows it. Anyhow, she thinks you're sweet and lovely. She told me so."

He added:

"And my stepfather said you were a poppet and extremely beautiful. So natural—he doesn't really like all that terrific make-up Franny goes in for—the false eyelashes and the rest of it. But you mustn't mind Franny. She doesn't mean half she says or does. She's quite unique."

Cressida did not argue the point although she felt that Franny meant everything she said that was at all unpleasant.

After Cressida had been to the lovely house in Hampstead several times, she learned a few more unattractive truths about Sam's mother. For instance, that she had in the past held it against her own son because his father's Will had been made in favour of Sam rather than herself. That, Cressida felt sure, had been done because Martin Paull had realised how unscrupulous his wife was about money. Just as poor old Sir Guy was beginning to realise it. Also, Cressida gathered that both Franny and the trustees had kept Sam short of money, both at school and afterwards when he was up at Cambridge.

In fact Sam had had rather a hard time. His wealthy stepfather had arrived on the scene too late to give a helping hand. It was his father's brother, Uncle Richard, who had made it possible for the boy to go on to the Stock Exchange.

All these things in turn swayed Cressida towards Sam and against Lady Fennell. She felt that he needed her. Handsome, attractive to other women he might be, but there was a 'little boy lost' quality in him which roused Cressida's compassion, and finally her love.

Little by little he also made her feel that he was necessary to *her*. So there came the night following one of Franny's little dinner parties when Cressida finally wrenched from her heart that first destructive love and replaced it with Sam's. Sam's wonderful love that could give as well as take.

That night when they left the house, Cressida was in a particularly warm, sweet mood. Both Franny and old Guy had been exceptionally nice to her tonight.

"Why not?" he had asked and took one of her hands and brushed his lips against it. "You're a darling person, Cressida. They know now that I am in love with you and they hope you are going to marry me."

For the first time that Sam could remember, Cressida did not draw away from him at the mention of the word *marriage*. Hope made him optimistic. On the way back to Brighton, he turned the car into a quiet by-road and took her into his arms.

"When are you going to say 'yes' to me, Cress? I do love you so much, darling. We have known each other for nearly four months now. I know it isn't very long, but it all seems a hell of a long time to *me*. I want you so badly, my darling."

All the bitterness, the loneliness, the pain that had been hers when she first left Rome, seemed suddenly to recede into the shadows and stay there. She wanted so much to know what it was to be happy again. She wanted to be loved and she wanted to *love*. That was the main thing. She wanted to be able to love, instead of feeling cold and bitter.

She put her arms around his neck and drew his cheek down to hers.

"Oh Sam, you are so wonderful to me. You *couldn't* be nicer."

He tasted the salt of tears as he turned his lips to hers.

"Darling, you are crying. Have I upset you? I know I promised not to go on pestering you, but—"

"I don't mind," she broke in and for a moment she sobbed helplessly, hugging him, feeling that she had suddenly sailed into harbour out of the storm. She felt secure with Sam. Security was so important.

"I am crying because I know now that I love you," she said and then laughed and cried together.

"You love me. Have you changed your mind then?" he asked incredulously.

"Yes, I have and I want to marry you."

"God, how wonderful," he exclaimed. She felt her heart suddenly lift. The ghosts of the past vanished completely leaving her with a sensation of such exquisite relief that her whole being yearned towards Sam. She took his warm face between her hands and kissed him on the mouth.

"I don't know why you want me. I don't think I am the right girl for you, but you seem to think I am so that's that. I'll try to be everything that you want, I *want* to be. I'm so grateful for your love."

"You are everything to me, Cress. I adore every hair of your head."

"You shouldn't adore anybody. It doesn't pay."

"Don't say things like that. When you're bitter you scare me. One of the things that has mystified me most about you is that you seem so disillusioned at times. You behave as though you can't trust any man."

40

She leaned her face against his shoulder and shut her eyes.

"I won't feel like that any more. I won't. You've given me back my faith and trust. I know that you are completely to be trusted, Sam darling."

"This is marvellous," he said joyfully, "this is what I have been praying for and never dared believe would happen. Cress—I swear I'll make you the happiest girl in the world. That is if you will forgive my shortcomings."

"I've yet to find any."

"You know that's not true. I'm a very ordinary fellow. *You're* the extraordinary one."

"Please don't idealise me, please don't."

"I've done so long ago—you're too late," he laughed.

"Oh Sam," she said, "You make me feel so humble. I really think I ought to tell you—"

"I don't want you to tell me anything except that you love me," he interrupted. "I know someone hurt you long ago, but to hell with them. I'm going to prove to you that love needn't hurt. I won't let mine hurt you—ever."

She took one of his long, well-shaped hands and put her lips against it.

"I'm sure it won't. You couldn't hurt anybody, Sam. I really do love you. I may only have just realised it tonight, but I think I've loved you for ages."

"In that case, you'll agree we shouldn't waste any *more* time," he said. "Next month—July—we'll get married. A month from now—if you're willing, Cress. No more waiting about. Agreed?"

She nodded. Once again she experienced that strange sense of relief of being sure that here was a man she could trust and love for all her life.

She reached up and kissed him.

"Anything you say, boss," she whispered, and her lips trembled and her eyes filled with tears which he quickly kissed away.

It was a memorable night. By the time they got back to the bungalow, Sam had already slipped a ring on to her finger, the diamond and ruby his mother had given him for his future wife. The next day they were formally engaged.

4

ONCE Sam had pinned his Cressida down, even to fixing the date for an early wedding at the end of July, he did not relax his efforts to make her feel she had done the right thing.

Her father liked Sam immensely and Freda, having accepted Sam, adored him and called him 'the splendid lover'. He looked, she said, rather like an Austrian, with his big, athletic figure, his fair hair and his bright blue eyes.

Austrian or English—it would have been all the same to Cressida. She had begun to admire and respect the young man in earnest. He had gathered her to him with a lovely enveloping warmth which had melted the armour in which she had encased herself after Rome.

She turned her full capacity for loving towards him. It wasn't at all the same as it had been in Rome with Dominic, but she didn't want it to be. Only a fool would wish to be badly hurt twice in this life. The lightning that had struck and withered her would not strike again. Sam's love was not like that murderous flash. It was pure sunshine—sweet and healing.

She began to feel deeply ashamed of herself for the weakness in Rome. Dominic had broken her heart into tiny pieces. Sam had put it together again.

He was patient and understanding when sometimes she went down into the depths—which she still did, although only on rare occasions which grew more infrequent as time went on.

He used to call these dark moods her 'blackouts'. But he did not question her because he considered it wrong to pry into another human being's private inner life.

One night when they were talking together, he admitted that he realised there had been another man in her life—an affair that must have been unhappy and even embittering. She immediately retired behind a shutter of silence and secrecy after which he said no more. He was so completely in love he did not want to take any risk of pushing her away—losing her confidence.

Things were quite good for Sam, financially, at the present stage of his life. But Sam often made it obvious to Cressida that he had appreciated the fact that money was not of the same importance to her that it was to his mother. He was delighted because Cressida liked him to buy her a beautiful piece of glass or china rather than diamonds.

For the same reason, Cressida admired him. All men had to earn their living. It was Sam's job to buy and sell on the Stock Market and pay a good deal of attention to finance. But he was not mercenary and sport was of greater interest to him than material acquisitions.

He had a small Triumph-Herald, these days, in which he could pilot his Cressida around, and he merely laughed when his mother intimated that he had done a bad thing for himself in choosing a poor wife. He could, as she said, have lived a far more luxurious life with Diana, who was wealthy in her own right. But it was Cressida he loved—Cressida who could bring him nothing but herself. He loved her parents too. The big jolly Austrian mother, and the kindly doctor father whose life and health had been ruined, but who never complained. Let Franny turn up her nose at them and at the Brighton bungalow. Sam was satisfied.

Franny who adored organising and being the centre of attraction had wanted the wedding to take place in London where she, herself, could hold the reception and impress all her friends. But Cressida's mother had turned down the offer politely but a little indignantly.

"Cressida's father and I have saved a little for our daughter's wedding. It must take place from her own home," she declared.

Both Cressida and Sam enthusiastically agreed. The last thing they wanted was a huge social gathering of smart people.

So the wedding was going to be quite small. There would only be a few close friends as guests on both sides down in Brighton. Dr. Raye could not give his daughter away because of his wheelchair, which distressed him. But his brother, William Raye, a dental surgeon, who lived in Staffordshire, was going to come along and take his place at the wedding. Cressida felt sad about this, but fortunately she liked Uncle Bill. Of course, Sam's Uncle Richard Paull and *his* family

43

would be coming. Betty and Geoffrey Chalmers, and several of Sam's friends too, would be among the guests.

The wedding was to take place at half past eleven on the last day of July in the little church of St. Albans which was not far from the bungalow. They had only to go down the hill to find themselves in Kemp Town which was at the Black Rock end of Brighton. St. Albans was halfway down the hill from the bungalow. Freda insisted on having a marquee on the lawn and had called in a firm of caterers to do the food. It was all arranged.

Uncle Bill's daughter Vicky and Betty Chalmers' schoolgirl sister-in-law, Julia were Cressida's bridesmaids. They had all had a lot of fun teasing her brother, Simon, threatening to dress him up as a page. He had in turn threatened to pour a bottle of ink over Cressida's wedding gown if they carried *that* joke much further.

Cressida was very fond of her young brother and delighted because Sam said that in the school holidays Simon could stay with them whenever he liked. Not only would it be good for Simon, but give her parents a chance to be quiet and alone together which a busy family life had so far denied them.

In defiance of superstition, Cressida had chosen green for the bridesmaids. The long full dresses were a delicate shade of almond green silk, with low necks and long tight sleeves. Both girls had blonde hair and would carry posies of lilies of the valley, with the same flowers in their hair. Cressida had chosen yellow roses for her own bouquet. They were her favourite flowers. It would be really a 'spring wedding'. Even Freda, in deference to her daughter's wishes, was wearing a yellow brocade suit and a big yellow hat with green trimmings.

There was some hitch about the Best Man. Sam had chosen a young stockbroker friend of his with whom he often worked —Tim Wilson. Tim had unfortunately been involved in a car smash, a fortnight ago. His right leg had been injured and there was now considerable doubt as to whether he would be capable even of hobbling to the wedding.

They were waiting to see.

Cressida had meant to ask her fiancé over the telephone just now the latest news about Tim's progress, but she had forgotten.

Soon after half past seven Sam drove up to the bungalow.

The July day had been lovely, but earlier in the afternoon storm clouds gathered over the Downs and by the time Sam got down to Brighton it was pouring with rain, and cooler.

Cressida had changed out of a cotton frock into a light wool dress. She was always careful to make herself look glamorous for Sam. He was quick to admire her this evening as he climbed out of the little Herald and saw her in the doorway. She smiled at him. What a big boy he was, she thought, towering above her. The weather never worried Sam. He was the healthiest person she knew. He strolled through the rain as slowly as though the sun was shining, which amused her. In the sitting room Sam caught both Cressida's hands, and held her a little apart.

"I won't touch you. You look too luscious. I like your hair swept up on one side like that."

Her long greenish eyes narrowed, laughing at him.

"You've got raindrops running down your face. Your hair shines and you look like a Viking."

"Do I gather that we like the look of each other ?"

"I do."

"So do I," he said on a more serious note, "Oh darling, isn't life marvellous ? We haven't many days to go now. I can't wait."

"Have you got our tickets ?"

He let go of her hand and drew a packet from his pocket. She looked at him with the pleasure that his appearance always gave her. Large and strong though he was, he did not appear unwieldy. He wore nice suits, and wore them well, and she liked his choice of ties. She knew that one he was wearing tonight. *She* had given it to him. He had said at the time that she was one of the few women he knew who could chose a tie that a man would like to wear.

"Here you are," he said and held the tickets out for her inspection.

Two airline booklets. *London to Majorca*. Neither of them had been to Majorca. It would be hot there and they could roast in the sun on the beach, and swim, and lie out in the hotel gardens. Sam had no intention of economising over his fortnight's honeymoon. They were staying at The Formentor, one of the loveliest hotels in Majorca.

Cressida felt really excited as she handed the tickets back to her fiancé.

"Oh what fun it will be! I feel quite dizzy at the thought!" she exclaimed.

"I won't tell you how dizzy the whole idea makes yours truly," said Sam, smoothing back his damp fair hair. He drew a packet of cigarettes out of his pocket and handed it to her.

She shook her head.

"No thanks, Sam Paull, you are in the dog-house."

"What have I done?"

"You haven't kissed me."

"Darling—I repeat what I said just now. You look too luscious. That lovely hair-do and your white wool dress and those jet earrings—most seductive against your pale skin. You smell good, too. I'm not going to kiss you. Once I start, I couldn't stop."

She laughed.

"You *are* absurd."

"Besides," he added, "I have got news for you."

"The wedding's off," she prompted.

"No, you bet your life it's not. But poor old Tim won't be our Best Man. He's sunk. Some infection has started up in the old leg and they're operating tomorrow morning. He won't even *get* to the wedding. He's very fed up, I assure you. I spoke to him on the phone. He sent you his love and all kinds of apologies and says the thing he most minds is that he won't be there to kiss the bride which is always the Best Man's privilege once we get to the vestry."

"Oh, I *am* disappointed," said Cressida and meant it. Tim was an endearing person, plumpish, red-headed, freckled and with a wonderful sense of humour. Like Sam, he was a Rugby football enthusiast and had in his time played in International Matches. Sam was devoted to him.

Cressida and Sam stood arm-in-arm for a moment by the open french windows looking out at the garden and chatting. The rain was still falling, drenching the roses. The sky was sad. Cressida suddenly felt sad—about Tim.

46

"What a shame," she sighed, "who will you ask now?"

"Well, I might have been in a bit of a quandary," Sam said, lighting his cigarette, "but by a very strange coincidence, an alternative was put on my plate just before I left the office."

"Tell me," said Cressida and rubbed her cheek fondly against his shoulder.

"A chap has turned up out of the blue. He was a very close friend of mine at Cambridge—as a matter of fact one of the most interesting characters I've ever met—*and* most generous. But there's a story about him that I must tell you sometime. It'll show you what a decent fellow he is. I'd rather played the fool my second year at Selwyn and got myself into debt. A bit like our Franny for once. I'd spent more than I had."

"That doesn't sound like you," said Cressida.

"Well it isn't really, but it happened on this occasion. We all have our weak moments, sweetie."

"Ageerd. And your friend helped out, did he?"

"He did and would have done a lot more if I had let him. He was grand about it. We were complete opposites—not like Tim and myself who agree on most things. Dom and I rarely saw eye to eye yet we got on well in a funny way—like opposites sometimes do. He didn't play games and I think he had a secret admiration for me because I got to the top that way. I'm not artistic and I admired him because he was the hell of a good artist. He could draw anybody. He did a sketch of one of the Dons that was a masterpiece. It's hanging up in Selwyn now, as a matter of fact."

Silence.

Sam turned and looked down at Cressida. She had drawn her arm away from his. He thought she looked odd.

"What's up, darling? I don't think you have been listening."

She didn't speak. Her heart was beating so violently that she thought she might faint. She walked away from Sam and sat down on the edge of one of the armchairs, gripping the sides with both hands. She said:

"Yes, I've heard everything, but—"

Before she could say more, he went on giving her his news.

"Dom and I were very good friends. Then he left Selwyn the year before I did. His people lived in Brazil. He was only half English. I lost touch with him. I think once he sent me a card from some mid-European port. He was always a restless type—always travelling around. I think it's a pity he had so much money because if he had had to earn his living he could have done it with his painting. He was really terrifically good. You should have seen his work. You know so much about art—you would have appreciated it, Cress."

She stared blindly at him. She heard her own voice as from a distance.

"Yes I would, wouldn't I?"

"Darling, you do look strange," he began.

"Go on telling me about this man," she said in a breathless voice.

"Well, his name's Dominic Miln. We all called him Dom. It's fantastic really that he's chosen just this moment to arrive in London. He's staying at some club or other. He looked up my stepfather's address, phoned there and they gave him my office number. It was just that he wanted to contact me again. He was keen on me going out and around town with him tonight, but I told him I was engaged."

Cressida felt as though all the heat in her body had departed. She was bitterly cold and trembling. Dominic was in London. *Dominic* had come back into her life—just like that! And Dominic by some fantastic coincidence knew Sam; had been up at Cambridge with him.

"It's all worked out wonderfully," continued Sam with his usual enthusiasm, blue eyes sparkling. "As I told Dom, he's arrived in the nick of time. I asked him if he would take Tim's place and be my Best Man next Saturday, and he said 'yes, of course.'"

Now Cressida's stricken gaze met Sam's. She looked positively horrified.

"He's going to be the Best Man?"

"Yes. But you'll like him—I promise. You two ought to have a lot in common."

"Oh, my God," said Cressida under her breath.

Sam grinned at her. He hadn't heard what she said.

Then Freda walked into the room followed by the doctor in his wheelchair.

5

WHILE Cressida and Sam ate their dinner at English's Oyster Bar where Sam had ordered a dish they both liked—Lobster *Americaine*—Cressida had established two important facts. First, that Sam did not know that she had already met Dominic Miln and, second, that it had become his dearest wish now to have Dominic as Best Man.

"I didn't want to be late driving down," he said, "It only struck me once I'd said good-bye to Dom that I hadn't told him the name of my bride-to-be . . ." he laughed. "Never mind—I'll be seeing him in town tomorrow. We're lunching together. I'll tell him then."

Cressida made a snap decision at least to inform Sam that she had met Dominic Miln. It would be quite ridiculous—and wrong—to pretend she didn't know him. She wanted to add that she didn't like him and didn't want him to come to her wedding. But that would have needed too much explaining. She would soon find herself floundering in a sea of difficulties. Sam finally made it impossible for her to express a dislike of Dominic. He said:

"When I heard Dom's voice again I realised how pleased I am that he got in touch with me. Now that Tim's out of it, I couldn't want anybody I like better than Dom at the wedding. I have never forgotten that time he got me out of my difficulties at Cambridge. I'm still very much in his debt, although, of course, I paid the actual money back long ago."

Cressida made no comment. Usually she enjoyed eating lobster at English's with Sam, who was very fond of his food and good at ordering special meals. Tonight she had no appetite. She had to force herself to eat at all. The last thing she wanted was to worry Sam or give herself away. She knew that if he could guess at the chaos in her mind, it would greatly distress him. Hearing Dominic's name again and from *this* particular quarter, and only a week away from her wedding day, had shocked her badly.

She thought that she had learned to blot out the past. She had thought herself capable of thinking about Dominic—when she allowed herself to think—coolly, painfully, perhaps, but she had believed she could stand apart from the pain and not allow it to govern her as it had done at first. Besides, since her engagement to Sam, she had grown genuinely, sincerely fond of him. More than that. The physical side in her had been roused again, and she needed Sam as a lover as well as a friend. She had no intention of letting him feel at all cheated. She *wanted* him to make love to her, and she was willing and eager to respond.

Now, if she wasn't careful she would tumble catastrophically down the hill that she had climbed so steadily once Sam had come into her life.

It would be all right, she thought miserably, if she could only tell Sam to stop talking about Dominic and not on any account to renew the old friendship. Most certainly she wanted to ask him not to allow Dominic to play such an important part at her wedding.

But the more Sam talked, the plainer he made it that he was bent on Dominic being Best Man and absolutely delighted by the idea of renewing the old friendship. It all made things doubly hard for Cressida to be frank.

Sam always bubbled over with good spirits and enthusiasms. This very trait added to Cressida's difficulties. He kept praising Dominic—'old Dom' as he called him discussing his talents and his various characteristics. He didn't seem to notice Cressida's silence or the fact that something was radically wrong with her this evening. Perhaps that was because she didn't often raise those wonderfully expressive eyes of hers to his. She lowered her lashes and sipped her wine, or toyed with her food, and just put in a word or a nod, now and then.

But she felt she would *die* if Sam kept talking about Dom.

"I must get him to do a drawing of you as soon as we come back from our honeymoon!" Sam said with an ardent look at her. *He* really did like those jet earrings against her lovely camellia-white skin, *he* thought admiringly.

"I'd like him to paint you in that green dress you wore the other night—you remember—at Franny's? An emerald green chiffon, wasn't it, with a satin belt? It made your waist look tiny and Franny said the colour matched your eyes. I forgot to tell you, incidentally, that she said your eyes were as green as a cat's. I assured her that's as far as it goes because there is nothing catty about my Cressida."

Cressida put down her knife and fork and covered her lips with her table-napkin. Her hands were shaking. She felt sick. She could hear Dominic's rather high caressing voice:

"Little Cat . . . My Little green-eyed Cat."

Really, I will go mad she told herself, *if Sam goes on like this.*

But poor Sam, not realising the frenzy to which he was driving his loved one, continued praising her beautiful green eyes and expressing his wish for Dom to paint her.

Now, Cressida thought to herself, *it's time I did something . . . said something.*

She gulped some of the iced hock that the waiter had just poured out for her. Without looking at Sam, she spoke:

"Darling, you've been talking so much you haven't given me time to tell you *my* news."

They were sitting side by side on a little sofa. He laid a hand on her knee.

"Sorry, sweetie. How remiss of me. I do talk too much when I get worked up, don't I? But I can't tell you what a lot of pleasure it's given me getting Dom back in my life just at this psychological moment."

She shut her eyes. She could have laughed if it hadn't all been so painful—even tragic. Psychological moment. Oh, God—yes! But why did Dominic of all men in the world who had once been so important to Sam up at Cambridge come back into Sam's life today. Sam was just the sort of faithful, trusting, affectionate person who would never forget a kindness—or a friendship. She could quite understand how he would feel about the man who once had been generous to him. Just as she understood about Dominic helping Sam. That was in keeping with *his* generous nature. But how little

Sam would have approved of that other side of Dominic, had he known. The ruthless egotistical side to a man who could live with a girl for as long as it suited him—then irrespective of how greatly it hurt her—fade out of her life. Sam, of all people, wouldn't approve of that sort of thing. Not he, with his old-world respect for women. Dear God! It would amaze and wound him, perhaps mortally, to learn that she and Dominic . . .

She dragged her thoughts away from the past—*that side* of it. She carried out her plan of campaign in this secret battle.

"It may surprise you to know that I have already met your wonderful Dom," she said.

Sam's very blue eyes sparkled at her. He brushed the thick fair curling hair back from his forehead with a characteristic gesture.

"Not true! *You* know old Dom ?"

"Yes," she said steadily, "we met in Rome. You remember I went there as an *au-pair* girl a year ago."

"Yes, but how absolutely grand, darling. Of course Dom would have been thrilled if I'd mentioned your name on the phone, but there was no time. I just asked him if he would be my Best Man and left all the details for our lunch tomorrow."

Cressida thought:

I wonder what Dominic will do when he hears who the bride actually is . . . He might cry off. I can only pray to God he does !

She didn't want to see him again. She didn't. *She didn't*.

"Tell me all about where and how you met Dom. Didn't you find him fascinating ?" asked Sam, pouring out some more wine for her.

"Yes."

"You know about how well he paints, then ?"

"Yes. He had a studio in Rome at the time I was there. He came to the house where I was working, to sketch the Duchessa's two children. That's how we met."

"He hasn't turned professional ? He said he never would."

"No. His mother and the Duchessa were friends and he sketched the children just to please the Duchessa."

"I bet," said Sam with a grin, "that if the Duchessa was young and beautiful he was palavering with her. Old Dom could never resist a palaver with a pretty woman. He used to be a terror at Cambridge."

Cressida sat still. Her thoughts, her memories whirled like little blind stricken birds from one side of her brain to the other . . . or so it seemed.

She knew only too well how the young Dominic, as an undergraduate, would behave. Thoroughly badly with girls. She could even believe that Dominic *had* 'palavered' as Sam put it, with the Duchessa although he had never admitted it to *her*.

"Did you see much of him?" asked Sam.

She kept her gaze lowered and prayed for forgiveness as she told a bare-faced lie.

"No—only on and off."

"Did you see many of his paintings?"

"Yes."

"What did you think of them?"

"I think, as you do, that he is frightfully clever and it is a pity he didn't *have* to paint. He only seemed to get spasmodic periods of wanting to express himself on canvas. With all that money, of course, he was able to rush round the world in a sort of playboy way—which distracted him from his work."

"Yet he wasn't really a playboy. At least not in my view—up at Cambridge," said Sam. "He had a very serious side, old Dom. Too serious for me—philosophy and all that. He used to go to meetings I would have found madly boring."

She knew. She knew every single thing that Sam had to tell her about Dominic. She sat there feeling helpless, the captive of her own too-vivid imagination.

Sam had so much to say about his old Cambridge friend. He wanted to know this and that about Rome; Cressida's opinion of Dom out there. Finally, Cressida felt unable to bear any more and changed the conversation.

"I made that appointment as you asked me with the electrician at Cowfold. He's going to meet us there on Friday to put the wall-lights up in the sitting room."

"Good," said Sam, ready and willing to forget Dom and turn his thoughts to his future home. Then he noticed suddenly how little Cressida had eaten of her lobster.

"Wasn't it good, darling?"

"Yes, but I'm not hungry tonight."

"Would you like some fruit or a savoury?"

"No nothing more, just coffee."

"I'm going to have a savoury."

"You do that," said Cressida and smiled at him feeling warmly affectionate. He was such a darling. So completely natural. Healthy and hungry and without inhibitions. *Dear God, if only she could be the same!*

Damn Dominic for coming back into her life. She had been so certain that she had laid that ghost and here it was creeping back to torment her. She hated Dominic. She hated the memory of all there had been between them. It seemed wrong now—unfair to the man she was going to marry. Yet she hadn't felt that way at the time. And she didn't *really* hate him—that was absurd, of course. But one certainly couldn't go on adoring the person who had carved one's heart up into little pieces!

She felt dreadfully tired. Soon after the coffee, she asked Sam to take her home.

As they drove along the Brighton front—it was not a nice night but was still drizzling—towards the road that led up to the bungalow, Sam re-opened the subject of Dominic.

"He'll be frightfully interested when I tell him the name of my fiancée, won't he?"

"Yes," said Cressida and clenched her hands in her lap.

"There isn't much time now for you two to get together before the wedding, but I could bring him down to dinner one night—" began Sam.

"No, don't," she said sharply.

In the dusk of the car she could sense rather than see Sam throw her a puzzled look.

"Why, darling?"

She stammered:

"I—I'm so busy—I'm going to be terribly busy till Saturday now. Mummy and I are doing a lot of sewing and packing —I'll see Dominic on the Great Day."

"O.K. darling," said Sam cheerfully.

She laced and unlaced the fingers in her lap. She was seized by a terrible temptation to tell Sam everything. He loved her so much, she was sure he would forgive her. After all he wasn't *all that* old-fashioned. It wouldn't seem the end of the world because she and Dominic had had a mad, passionate affair in Rome.

Or—for Sam—*would it be the end*? He was an idealist in his way. She knew quite well that he idealised her. He was always telling her so. He trusted her absolutely and was confident about her love for him. Wouldn't it hurt him dreadfully if she destroyed that belief and wouldn't it mean complete disillusionment for him in his old friend? It was all so tricky. Cressida began to feel so confused that she could no longer think straight. By the time Sam drove the car up to the bungalow, she had made up her mind that she couldn't and wouldn't tell him the whole truth. It would be too unkind to him. She, herself, might benefit, but would it be fair, just to relieve her own conscience? She remembered talking to Mummy only the other day about some woman they both knew who had had an illicit love affair and told her husband about it, and Mummy had said that she thought the so-called luxury of confession should not be indulged in unless it could do good. What good could it do to Sam to tell him? On the contrary, it would be harmful.

The best thing was to let him go on thinking that she had known Dominic but not well and to put up with the awful business of seeing Dominic act as Sam's Best Man on Saturday. Of course, when Dominic heard her name, he might try to get out of it—he might not want to be at the wedding under the circumstances.

Yes, that was a hope; that Dominic would show some delicacy and tact and back out of being Best Man.

Suddenly she felt that she wanted terribly to contact Dominic before he met Sam for lunch tomorrow. He surely wouldn't be bad enough to give her away. She had never thought Dominic exactly the cad-type, ruthless though he was with his love affairs. In his own way, he had been honest with her; he had never promised marriage. She had, she supposed, *asked* to be hurt—she had been so madly, passionately in love. So weak.

But she would like to talk to Dominic before he saw Sam. As casually as possible she asked where Dominic was staying.

"If the occasion arose, I might phone him up myself and ask him down," she said and was conscious that she had already started to deceive Sam. It was horrible.

Unaware of her misery, he told her at once that Dom was staying at the Oxford and Cambridge University Club in Pall Mall. Sam was also a member there.

"Do ring him," said Sam innocently. "I am sure he would like to hear from you in person."

He held her in his arms and kissed her good night in the usual way—his lips first of all brushing hers gently, then clinging with growing passion. She could feel the beat of his heart against her breast, and all his urgent longing for her. She put her arms around his neck and responded with a passion that held a touch of desperation. She loved him so much. She did not want to hurt him. She was determined not to do so. He was such a good person and he had been so good to her. He was so much more worthwhile than Dominic Miln.

Oh damn, *damn* Dominic! She refused to let him upset her life and come between her and Sam by one single hair's breadth. The warmth of her response to Sam was greater than he had felt from her ever before.

He was delighted and said so.

"Darling—you're sweet. *Terrifically* sweet," and he held her small body so tightly against his that he hurt her.

The tears stung her eyelids.

"I do love you, Sam," she said brokenly.

He sensed that there was something different about her tonight, but could not guess what it was, and did not ask. It was enough for him that she really seemed to love him at last as much as he loved her.

For Cressida it was a bad night.

It was impossible for her to sleep without remembering everything that she had meant to forget—about Dominic.

She really did not know how to deal with the situation. In the early hours of the morning she switched on her table lamp, sat up in bed and tried to read a library book. But the pages and the print danced in front of her tired eyes. She felt quite stupid and sat disconsolately staring around her room which despite Mummy's efforts, was still untidy and crammed with all the paraphernalia of the coming wedding. In particular, she let her gaze rest a moment on her studio portrait of Sam which she kept in a leather frame beside her bed. The light showed up his fine features and broad shoulders; his square, strong chin; the sweetness of his humorous mouth. Dear, *dear*, Sam! She wasn't going to let him be hurt over this, whatever happened—that was the one clear thought in the confusion of her mind.

She got up early and went out into the garden. Her head throbbed and her eyes felt sore. This wouldn't do, she thought; she couldn't allow herself to be so upset by Dominic.

She walked for an hour over the Downs. The freshness of the summer morning and the beauty of the Sussex Weald, misty as yet, with dew spangling the green grass as though with a million crusted diamonds, did her good. She felt refreshed as she walked back into the bungalow and switched on the electric kettle.

As a rule it was Freda who was up early getting her husband some breakfast. This morning at the unusual hour of seven o'clock, Cressida took tea into her parents' bedrooms.

"I'm going to give you a treat and bring you your breakfast tray, Mum," she told the astonished Freda, who sat up in bed looking plump and rather young with her fair hair hanging around her shoulders. In the adjoining room, John Raye, his greying head buried in the pillow, was still asleep.

"Heavens!" exclaimed Freda, "What's come over you, Cressida, up and about at this hour?"

"I just couldn't sleep."

Freda eyed her daughter a trifle doubtfully. She was always pale, but this morning she looked too pale and languid-eyed, the mother reflected. Rather boyish in those blue linen jeans, check shirt, but how pretty she was, Freda's reflections ran on, fondly. Such slenderness and such grace, and with her dark hair and those wonderful slanting eyes that were all legacies from her father's family. Serious illness and long years of hard work had altered poor John sadly, of course. He was lined and emaciated these days, and looked twice his age.

But Freda could remember her husband when he was a dark, slim young man with Cressida's quiet charm and extreme good looks. As for those fantastic eyes and lashes—they were inherited from her grandmother. There was mixed blood in Cressida; not only was her mother an Austrian, but her father's mother had come from Russia.

It had been a war romance. John's father met the beautiful Russian girl with the green eyes in a hospital where he was working with the R.A.M.C. and she was a V.A.D. nurse. The rest of her family had been martyred in the Russian Revolution.

Simon showed none of the Russian strain. He might well have been English with his fair hair, snub-nose and freckles.

Freda was on the verge of asking Cressida if anything was wrong with her this morning, but restrained. She had learned that it was better not to ask too many questions. Cressida didn't like it. She was such a strange, secretive little thing. But she had been so much more affectionate since her return from Rome that Freda accepted the fact that her daughter was different from other girls—and at times incomprehensible.

Anyhow, it was a nice change to be waited on and Freda appreciated the coffee and toast when Cressida brought the tray in later with the morning paper.

Having done her good deed, the girl returned to the kitchen to drink her own coffee, then she wrestled with herself on the subject of Dominic.

She felt still quite unable to accept the idea of Dominic being Best Man at her wedding. She kept changing her mind. First of all, she would ring him—then she wouldn't. Then she would. The palms of her hands felt a little damp, the more she thought about it.

What a thing to have happened! It couldn't be more awkward. She had hoped the past was over and done with. It *wasn't* that she still loved Dominic, of course. She was sure that she loved Sam—with all her heart and soul. But Dominic had once meant a great deal and only six months ago—she wouldn't have been human if she hadn't felt some repercussion from the pain—and the ecstasy.

"I just don't want him back in my life," she said the words

aloud, while she stirred her coffee and looked blindly around Mummy's model kitchen.

This room was the one luxury Freda had allowed the doctor to pay for when they moved here, and a very pretty kitchen it was with blue and white units and blue vinyl-floor and the long low picture window through which the sun was streaming this bright July morning.

A blue-tit hopped on to the window ledge—pecked at a piece of old toast Freda had put out. The birds in this garden were lovely. Cressida adored watching them. But this morning she did not watch the pretty little bird.

She had been so happy with Sam since their engagement. She didn't want anything to spoil it now. They had grown so close. She had thoroughly enjoyed these last few weeks getting their little house ready; getting to know each other's tastes and ideas; learning to give and take, and accept their differences of temperament and outlook, for, of course, there were many. But this was what marriage would mean—this effort to see eye to eye and tolerate each other's short-comings. She was sure that most of the short-comings were hers—Sam was always so unselfish and loving.

"I won't let Dominic upset Sam—or me!" Cressida said the words aloud and walked out into the hall and sat down at the telephone.

She dialled London and the number of Dominic's club.

When she heard his voice—it was so familiar and yet seemed like the echo from another life—her heart lurched. She was at once angry with herself because of the lurch. She had no right to let his voice have the slightest effect upon her.

"Hello," she said.

"Hello—who is that?"

"You don't recognise me," she said with a short laugh. And she was angry with herself again for minding that he had not recognised her.

An instant's silence, then Dominic said:

"*Mamma mia!* . . . Cressida . . . the *Little Cat!*"

She was furious now—not with herself but with him for daring to use that name. She trembled.

"Yes, it's Cressida."

"*Mamma mia !*" he repeated.

His favourite ejaculation in Italian. She had heard him use it hundreds of times.

"Where on earth have you sprung from and how on earth did you know where I was!" he added, with astonishment.

"I'm in my home in Brighton and I knew where you were because *Sam* told me."

"Sam who ?" he began, then: "Not Sam *Paull* ?"

"Yes. I'm the one who is being married to him on Saturday."

Another silence followed by a low throaty laugh which ended in a cough.

"Sorry, darling. Smoking too much."

How dared he call her *darling*, she asked herself.

"You could knock me down with a feather," he went on. "*You* are the bride-to-be. Good God! I spoke to old Sam yesterday and he asked me to be his Best Man."

"Exactly—and I'm phoning to tell you that I don't want you to be," she said.

"Now wait a minute. Don't let's fly off the handle."

"I'm not flying off anything, Dominic. I just think that under the circumstances you oughtn't to be Sam's Best Man."

"Why not ?"

She felt her cheeks colour.

"Aren't you rather insensitive ?"

"What should I be sensitive to ?"

"*Really*, Dominic !"

"Some months ago we had a love affair in Rome. Does that exclude me from being your future husband's Best Man now ? I knew him long before I knew you, you know."

"That may be."

"He's terribly keen for me to do the job, and I said I would, because his other friend has gone to hospital."

"That's true, but I still don't think—"

"Look, my dear," broke in Dominic. "I don't think we can discuss this on the telephone. We had better meet."

"No," she said, "I don't want to meet you."

"Aren't you being a little dramatic ?"

"Aren't you being wilfully dense—or don't you really understand how I feel ?" she asked indignantly.

"Cressida, darling, what happened between us is over and done with."

So, she thought bitterly, it hadn't really meant much to *him*. She had known that all along. He was heartless. For him it had just been 'a love affair'—one of dozens.

"Cressida," he said, "I dare say you have cause to dislike me and I have always disliked myself for what I did to you. I was a bloody awful coward and I'm not in the least proud of the way I behaved. But I wasn't as unfeeling as you imagine. I really wanted to see you again, but I thought it would be less upsetting then if I didn't, also that the break would be quicker and more final if we didn't meet. If I was wrong, I'm sorry."

The ghosts of the past were crowding back on her now with a vengeance. She felt suffocated and confused. But out of the confusion the sensation of bitter resentment was uppermost.

"What you did was unpardonable, but I'd rather not discuss it, please."

"I'm sorry, Little Cat," his voice sounded very gentle and apologetic now.

"It's all over," she said. "Sam is the only person that matters."

"Right. We agree on that. Sam is the only person that matters and he wants me to be his Best Man."

"But you can't want to be," she exclaimed incredulously.

"Oh, yes I do. I've always been devoted to old Sam. Incidentally, he's one of the best—you've made a wise choice."

"I know that," she said.

"I don't as a rule like these functions," went on Dominic, "but Sam tells me it's going to be a very quiet wedding and I thought it might be a nice gesture on my part as he and I were such good friends at Cambridge. That, of course, was before I knew the name of the bride. Now that I do know, I'm even more interested."

"I just don't understand you!"

"Darling, you are being very old-fashioned. You dramatise things much too much."

She thought that if he were standing there before her

instead of being at the other end of the telephone, she would have hit him. In order not to show her feelings, she had to clench her hands until the points of her nails hurt the palms.

"We don't see eye to eye on this, obviously," she said.

"You must be in love with Sam or you wouldn't be marrying him," said Dominic.

"That's true. I adore him. I think he is the most marvellous man in the world!" she said with passion.

"Then why let what happened between *us* matter so much after all this time?"

"You just don't understand," she said hopelessly.

"You're taking the conventional attitude," he went on, "you must remember that I was never one for convention."

"It's fantastic to me that you don't feel—more delicacy," she said, gulping.

She heard him laugh.

"Darling Cressida, how sweetly Victorian! What a lovely word, '*delicacy*'."

She didn't know what to say to him next. Of course she had seen this side of Dominic before—couldn't fail to know him having been so close to him, so much with him, while their affair lasted. She used to comment on his attitude towards various situations and laugh . . . for instance when he was being malicious, or witty, or clever at somebody's expense. And sometimes, of course, she had felt that he was incapable of understanding the feelings of others. He was so self-absorbed. It was only physical pain or distress that affected him, or the financial hardship of those less lucky than himself. He had always been a strange character—almost schizophrenic in his way.

She really did not know how to tackle him. She could see that he wanted her to behave as though nothing untoward had ever happened between them. She certainly didn't want to rake the ashes of the past too vigorously. But, because she was more vulnerable, she could not help being a little emotional about it all. Perhaps she *was*, as he said, too old-fashioned. Perhaps that was why her up-to-date and amoral conduct in Rome had reacted upon her so violently. She hadn't been really cut out for a promiscuous affair. It had had a murderous effect upon her whole being.

"Hello, are you there?" came from Dominic.

"Yes."

"I'm really awfully pleased to hear your voice again, you know, and I'm longing to see you, Cressida," he said softly.

She was defeated. She had never imagined that anybody could be so cool, so untouched by the past—the passion they had shared. She could certainly believe that it hadn't really hurt him at all to leave her. She could also see what a fool she had been to let it hurt *her* so much.

"Do you absolutely hate me?" she heard him ask and could swear that his voice held a touch of amusement.

It entered her mind now that if she went on being dramatic and emotional about this Best Man business, it would only flatter him and he might even begin to wonder if she still cared for him. That would be awful—*and* humiliating. Suddenly she changed her tune. To hell with what had happened in Rome. She wasn't going to let him think she cared a *damn*, any more.

"I don't in the least hate you," she said coldly and clearly. "I feel quite indifferent."

She heard his low well-remembered chuckle.

"Dear Little Cat—you haven't altered."

"I've altered a great deal and I really would rather you didn't go on using that ridiculous name."

"Sorry, Miss—er—Raye," he said with formality.

"Look here," said Cressida, "Let's get this straight, Dominic—you want to behave as though we were just casual friends in Rome. Very well. That's what you can tell Sam when *he* tells you who he's marrying."

"That's better," said Dominic, "I'd hate us to be enemies or for me to have to disappoint old Sam. So you won't go on objecting to me being Best Man?"

"It doesn't thrill me, but by all means do so if you wish— and, as you say—don't let's disappoint Sam."

"I'll try to act the part with grace," he said.

"I'm sure you will," she said icily.

"We'll have to call some kind of truce, darling—I mean,

Cressida. Sorry if I keep calling you 'darling'. Force of habit."

She felt an uncontrollable dislike of Dominic and yet when he went on to say how much he looked forward to seeing her again after six months she knew that in the depths of her heart she would like to see him again, too. She might despise him for what he once did to her, but all the way along she must have known what sort of person he was. Who could she really blame for the whole thing but herself? When she had heard about girls in similar situations hadn't she always criticised the woman who threw all the blame on the man? *She* after all, had thrown herself into Dominic's arms. It was for that idiocy she had paid and, anyhow, what did it all matter now? In a few days' time she would be Sam's wife.

"Are you well? Is all well with you?" Dominic asked just as though they were indeed two old friends who had met again—friends who need not look back in anger or reproach.

She decided to take her cue from him. After all, if she insisted on emnity, it must inevitably react badly on Sam.

"I'm fine, thank you, Dominic," she said, "and you—I mean—your mother—is she——?"

He broke in on the stammered inquiry.

"Poor little mother died a couple of months after we returned to Brazil. I was glad I went with her."

"Yes, of course. I'm sorry about your mother."

"I stayed on in Brazil for a month or so settling up our estate. Then I travelled for a bit. Then I decided it was time I stopped wandering around the world doing nothing and interested myself in quite a different form of art. Aldo Canletti —I expect you know who I mean—he's made a considerable name for himself as a scenic artist for Italian opera, asked me to design some sets for him. I joined up with him and worked with him in Florence. I didn't go to Rome," Dominic ended on a lower note, "whether you believe it or not I *did* feel a few qualms about going back there so soon. So, you see, I am not quite as insensitive as you may think."

That statement struck a chord in Cressida which alarmed her. She answered him sharply:

"Well, *I* certainly haven't been back to Rome and don't

64

intend to go. I'd had enough of the Duchessa and Italian society by the time I left."

"I'm afraid you might see more of me once you get back from your honeymoon," continued Dominic, "I know Sam will want to organise a few meetings. I've taken a flat in town as from the end of this week. I'm going to be in town working with Canletti on sets for the next opera season. I find it rather fascinating. I also find I'm quite good at it. I had a great success in Milan with my cathedral scene for Tosca the other day. We are bringing it over to London next month. It's really rather revolutionary."

"I'm sure it is, if you are at the back of it," said Cressida.

"Is that meant to be sarcastic?" he laughed.

"No, you know I have the highest regard for you as a painter," she said, "not that I know much about it. You taught me all I do know," she admitted.

"You were an excellent pupil, darl—I mean, Cressida."

She found him maddening and still too disturbing for her peace of mind. She turned the conversation to Sam.

"I'm terribly lucky, getting Sam for a husband. He's such a wonderful person."

"Well, as I have just agreed, I think he's tremendous, but you astonish me a little."

"Why?"

"You always told me you preferred the artistic type and that athletic men bored you."

"I've changed," she said in a haughty voice.

"Oh, well, I shall be most interested to see you again," he said.

"If you don't mind I must say good-bye," she said. "I just want to explain why I rang you up before Sam meets you today to tell you that I am the one he is engaged to. Just please don't mention that I phoned, will you? But I wanted you, if you *are* going to be Best Man to—to—" she broke off, floundering for words.

"To say that you didn't like me," he finished for her.

"No," she said, and her face was red. "What I wanted to explain is that Sam knows absolutely nothing about *us*."

"Darling," said Dominic, "if you think I am going to tell

him, I shall feel insulted. I'm everything that you like to think, but not *that* bad. I'il tell him what the film stars tell reporters. 'We are just good friends.' "

Her cheeks grew hotter.

"Thank you," she said stiffly. "Good-bye."

"Good-bye," said Dominic, "and please accept my very sincere congratulations—and good wishes for the wedding day. I must now go out and choose you a nice wedding present. Tell me what you need."

"Nothing," she said stupidly, "absolutely nothing."

She put down the receiver. She was thoroughly upset. The increased tempo of her heartbeats told her that. The whole conversation with Dominic had been most upsetting to her. She only wished that it hadn't been and that she could have felt as cool and unconcerned as he obviously did.

The last thing on earth she wanted was to see him at her wedding, standing beside Sam. Somehow it didn't even seem *decent*, although she supposed Dominic would have called that Victorian sentiment.

Freda, in dressing-gown, came into the hall carrying the breakfast tray.

"On the phone already," she beamed at her daughter, "Your sweet Sam, I suppose!"

"No," said Cressida. "Somebody else," and she fled before her mother could ask who it was.

6

THAT night, Sam was not coming down to Brighton as he had to attend a business dinner with his uncle in London. Cressida waited rather anxiously for a further telephone call from him. During the lunch hour she felt decidedly ill at ease, remembering that the two men who figured so largely in her life, were having lunch together.

She could only pray that Dominic would be discreet.

It seemed that he was. Soon after half past two, Sam telephoned Cressida.

"I thoroughly enjoyed my chop with old Dom. It was just like the old days at Selwyn. He hasn't really changed and he said I hadn't but I fancy that I have put on a bit of weight and that he's thinner."

"Oh, yes," said Cressida politely and was annoyed because she felt nervous.

Sam continued in his enthusiastic boyish way:

"Darling, it's terrific that you and old Dom know each other and that my Best Man won't be a stranger to you."

God, thought Cressida, a *stranger* . . . Dominic! . . . She wished Sam didn't like him so much. Somehow the reiterated name 'old Dom' vaguely irritated her. She supposed she was suffering from a guilt complex now. Maddening to think that she had been made to feel guilty just because Dominic had come back.

Sam went on talking; sad for old Dom, losing his beautiful mother; a pity he couldn't settle down anywhere; of course he was lucky having that huge estate in Brazil and so much money it wasn't true . . . etc., etc. To make matters worse for Cressida, Sam finished up with:

"Incidentally, darling, old Dom admires you a lot. He labelled you as 'unique' rather as I've always done. So you are, my precious!"

"Thanks, darling . . ." Cressida was fighting down her

irritation. She tried to steer the conversation away from Dominic.

"Shall I see you tomorrow, Sam?"

"You try not to see me," Sam laughed. "Twenty-four hours away from you is bad enough, forty-eight would asphyxiate me."

She had to laugh. Her mood lightened. It was so difficult to be depressed with Sam. He was as effervescent as champagne.

It was arranged that he would take her out to lunch in town tomorrow. She was going up to London for a final day's shopping. She still had some beachwear to buy for Majorca—and a new pair of sunglasses. Her own were broken. She remembered now that she had bought *those* in Rome. Just as well they were on the dust-heap . . . She wanted nothing to remind her of Rome, she thought almost viciously.

When she said good-bye to Sam, everthing seemed the same as it had been before Dominic arrived on the scene. She put him out of her mind.

Her mother left her in charge of the invalid that afternoon. Freda was going to tea with an old friend in Hove. She always left the bungalow under protest, but Cressida insisted.

"Once I'm married and gone you will be much more tied to Daddy. You get out while you can, Mummy. Though I will come over from Cowfold and take my turn—especially when Simon is home and you get really busy."

Freda kissed her daughter warmly.

"You're my sweet girl . . ."

"Not always so sweet," Cressida laughed and grimaced. "Look at the times I've been horrid and sour and disagreeable."

"Well, you've been very sweet lately," said Freda loyally.

"Sam's influence."

That, the mother thought, was probably true. Dear Sam had had a very good effect upon Cress. She wasn't nearly as moody or difficult as she used to be. Freda was sure that all was set for a very happy marriage. She was delighted.

After lunch, Cressida wheeled her father into the garden. The sun was quite hot today and there was little wind. They were sheltered by the one solitary tree which could be called a tree, at the end of the lawn. There was a swing seat there, too, with striped awning. Cressida curled up on the cushions with her needlework. She didn't care much for sewing, but she was taking great pride and pleasure in making one attractive lingerie set, herself. Today she had only to stitch the lace on to the bottom of the delicate shell-pink slip, and it would be finished.

Dr. Raye gazed at his daughter affectionately over the rims of his sunglasses. She looked very young, he thought, sitting like that with her legs tucked up under her. Such slim, brown legs. He hated the thought of losing her on Saturday, yet was so thankful that his Cressida seemed to have found real happiness. In his opinion, Sam Paull was a grand fellow and he felt no qualms about handing Cressida over to him.

"Trousseau about ready now?" he asked the girl affectionately.

"Yes, Daddy. London tomorrow and then two more days and it'll be my wedding eve. Hard to believe."

"It certainly is," said John Raye, sighed a little and nodded. "It makes me feel very old," he added, "having a married daughter!"

"Oh, you'll still have Simon. It's rather lucky he was born so long after me. He'll keep you and Mummy company when I'm away."

"Boys aren't the same as girls and I rather fancy my daughter," smiled John Raye and lit his pipe.

"I fancy my father," she said.

"I wish things had been easier for you, dear."

"Why do you say that?" she asked, sharply.

"I don't know—" Dr. Raye half closed his eyes and puffed at his pipe speculatively. "I never think you grew up with any ease. I mean you've never been an extrovert like your mother and Simon. They are the types who find life easy. You and I bottle things up. You've been through it—I know."

She looked at him with tenderness. He was old for his years, and lined and ill, although the doctors assured them that there was nothing to worry about and that he had many long years of life left to him. But Cressida could remember her father as the busy, bustling doctor who was wedded to his work. She could appreciate his present frustration. More than that—she could understand his inner loneliness despite the fact that he was never really left alone. Yes, she was like that, and she had always felt close to Daddy. For a moment she stopped sewing and looked across the hedge at the sloping Downs.

"You're quite right, Daddy," she said, "I don't think I did find it easy growing up, but I'm glad I didn't rush into marriage like some of my friends who got tied up in their late teens. Sam was worth waiting for."

"But there was somebody in Rome, wasn't there?"

He asked the question lightly, but it made her heart knock and her face grew scarlet.

"What makes you think so, Daddy?"

"I just know. Mind you, I've never so much as mentioned it to your mother. But I saw, when you first came home, that something had happened and imagined that it might be perhaps a love affair that didn't quite go right."

Cressida bit on her lower lip, jabbed the needle into the material—and into her own finger. She dropped her sewing with a little exclamation and sucked the tiny drop of blood that had appeared.

"So you *knew*," she said. "Darling Daddy, you certainly do keep things to yourself."

"Like you, Cress. But as it's so near your wedding day and I'm sure you're quite happy now, I felt a peculiar urge to mention it. I didn't want there to be any secrets."

"Well, I admit there *was* someone," she said with difficulty. "But it's all over, so you needn't worry."

"I don't. I *was* worried, obviously, but not any more."

"Then it's all right," she said. "Don't let's talk about the past. The present is so lovely."

John Raye took his pipe from his mouth and pressed a thumb into the bowl. Now suddenly, without warning or reason, he began to feel worried again. He almost wished he hadn't mentioned Rome to Cressida. He had seen that burning colour come to her cheeks and he didn't really like the way she shut up like a clam after admitting the affair. She didn't want to talk about it, and that seemed to him a bad sign. It must have been rather a poor show, or now, just about to be married to Sam Paull, surely she would have felt able to discuss it without concern?

The doctor made no further allusion to Rome. He began to talk about Majorca and Cressida's forthcoming honeymoon. Soon after that, Julia Chalmers, one of the bridesmaids-to-be, turned up, and the two girls went indoors to discuss the wedding. The invalid, left alone for a while, sat back on his cushions and dozed, the unsmoked pipe still between his fingers.

In her bedroom, showing young Julia some of her clothes and listening to her ecstatic praise, Cressida once again put the memory of Dominic right out of her mind.

It was absurd to go on like this, she thought. Nothing mattered now except her wedding day. And when Saturday came she was going to show Dominic how absolutely happy she was and defy even his presence at the ceremony to make a scrap of difference to her.

But her equilibrium was upset again when, only twenty minutes after Julia's arrival, another guest turned up at the bungalow. The two girls heard car wheels in the front drive and a scrunch of brakes on the gravel. They both looked out and stared rather wide-eyed at the big white Mercedes Benz, gleaming in the sunlight; then at the slim, young man in grey flannels who stepped out of it.

"Gosh! What a terrific car," began Julia with schoolgirl fervour, but Cressida looked at the Mercedes and the driver with no such enthusiasm.

Dominic! Oh, how *dared he* come down here?

She was forced to go out and meet him. He advanced, taking a packet of cigarettes from one pocket and a box of matches from the other, shaking it, to see if there were any matches left, so characteristic and familiar that it made her feel a trifle sick. She looked at the well-remembered face; he was very tanned; as usual, an untidy lock of dark hair fell across one eye. The dark, narrow eyes, smiled at her with all the old appraisal and criticism as though examining every detail of her.

"Cressida, my dear—" he began, how *are* you?"

"I—I—" she began to stammer and finished lamely: "How are *you*?"

"Fine. I left your—er—fiancé an hour and three-quarters ago. Not bad going from the City. We lunched in that new restaurant on the river. My car goes like a dream. I only got her yesterday. Ordered for me before I left Brazil. What do you think of her?"

"It's a s—splendid car," stuttered Cressida.

He was exactly the same as she remembered him except a little smarter and tidier than the rather untidy painter in his studio. He was being very natural, and treating her as though they were just old friends. Very well—that's exactly how she would treat him.

"Hope you don't mind me turning up like this without warning," said Dominic. "Sam felt sure I'd find you at home and that you might like to see me, and show me the church where you are being married, and so on."

"Yes, of course."

"Your people in?"

"Mummy's out. Daddy's in the garden. I'll take you out to meet him later."

Dominic lit his cigarette and glanced around the bungalow and the garden, then back at the girl.

"You're doing your hair a new way. I rather like it," he said, "it suits you."

His praise brought back her feeling of indignation that he was here. He saw her colour. He came up to her, took her right hand and put his lips against it.

"Don't be angry with me, Little Cat," he whispered.

The sheer insolence of the man made her gasp.

"Really, Dominic—"

"Well, I don't want you to hate me," he said, "I hate being hated. I admit that you have every reason to be angry with me, but do let's be adult over this show."

"Adult," she repeated the word rather bitterly.

"Well, it's over—our show, I mean," he went on. "And you're getting married to one of my best friends. Can't it rest at that?"

72

"By all means."

"Darling, I know you so well—I can see exactly how you feel about me, but I do beg you to be friends—that's all. I haven't wrecked your life, you know. It's pretty obvious, so why are you so furious with me?"

He took the wind out of her sails. She stood there, trembling a little—more angry with herself than with him. Then she forced a laugh.

"I'm not in the least furious. Let's stop being personal. Thank you very much for coming down to see me—it was good of you. And, of course, I'd like to show you the church. How's my Sam?"

"Your Sam's remarkably well. I envied him his appetite. He ate an enormous steak. As you'll remember, I never was one to eat much."

She nodded. She would rather not remember all their intimate little meals in their favourite Roman cafés; how she had commented out there on the fact that he ate so little for a man, and how for the first time, she had learned to drink and appreciate the red wine that he liked.

When Julia suddenly appeared, Cressida was thankful. She grabbed the younger girl's arm.

"Ju—meet Dominic Miln—Sam's Best Man who is replacing Tim."

"Hello," said Julia shyly and held out her hand. Dominic bent over it, almost but not quite touching it with his lips in the graceful Latin way he had with the opposite sex.

It was second nature to him to look with sensual interest at a pretty girl and Julia was very pretty in what he would call the conventional English style; fair hair; large dewy blue eyes; rather a nice figure—she was taller than Cressida and had long, sun-browned arms and legs. She looked attractive in her yellow cotton frock, touchingly young and fresh, Dominic thought. But the full pouting lips, bright pink, were inviting. Perhaps if Cressida hadn't been there, he might have offered to paint pretty Julia. She was an ideal Greuze, but he was for the moment interested only in his old love. Little Cat had matured vastly since they parted he considered. She was not so thin, but the camellia whiteness of her skin had all the old appeal for him like those fantastically beautiful eyes.

After seeing Sam again, Dominic had felt more than a little surprised that she had chosen to marry him—good fellow though he was. Dominic thought that she would have needed more finesse, more artistry in a lover.

She had been wonderful in Rome, he reflected as he followed the two girls into the bungalow. There had been a great many women in his life, but none had ever moved him to quite such tenderness as the Little Cat. He had found that mixture in her of temptestuous passion and virginal shyness so enchanting. He could almost regret that he did not fancy himself as a married man with a family. After leaving Cressida, he had missed her. That fact had profoundly astonished him.

Cressida looked out of the drawing-room window at her father's figure in the wheelchair. She knew from the way he was leaning back on the cushion that he was sleeping, and felt thankful.

"I won't take you out to Daddy—he needs rest," she told Dominic.

"Oh, of course," said Dominic and added with a twist of the lips: "I could never be called a restful character, could I?"

Julia Chalmers was looking at the visitor with open admiration. He asked if he could go along to the bathroom and wash his hands. After he had gone, Julia said:

"Ooh—isn't he *attractive*?"

Cressida raised her brows in a rather supercilious manner. "Is he?"

"M'm. *I'll* say so. Have you known him long? You've never produced him before. I suppose he's a friend of Sam's."

"Yes, they were at Cambridge together."

"What does he do now?"

"He paints in his spare time, but has some sort of stage-scenery job now for the opera. He is half Brazilian."

"Which accounts for the hand-kissing," said Julia nodding. "I must say I take kindly to him. Do you think I've got a chance? The Best Man is supposed to look after the bridesmaids. Now I've met him, I'm one up on your cousin Vicky. I must make myself very charming to him, or would you rather I left you alone, darling?"

"Whatever for?" Cressida almost snapped the question. "Please don't go. Stay to tea. I'm sure Dominic won't be here long. I'll just get him to run us down to the church. You can come too."

"I'd adore to," said Julia and hastily back-combed and put in place her thick fair hair and dabbed some powder on her retroussé nose. Cressida watched, feeling very much older than Julia. How nice to be eighteen, still naïve and untouched and inexperienced.

Julia added: "Simon will be back for the wedding, won't he?"

"Yes, he comes home tomorrow."

Her young brother had been in Devon since he left school for the summer holidays, camping at the sea with one of his school-friends.

Dominic returned.

"You must show me your home," he said, glancing at Cressida, "it looks delightful and what a wonderful position up here on the Downs. I could actually see the sea through your bathroom window."

"I'll go and make some tea," said Cressida hurriedly.

He tried to keep her in the room by saying that he didn't drink tea, but she insisted upon going in to the kitchen and leaving him alone with Julia.

With some slight malice she felt aware that Dominic wanted to talk to her alone and was annoyed with her because she wouldn't get rid of Julia.

Finally, when her father woke up, they all of them had tea out in the garden. Dominic was forced to join in a general conversation. Later Freda returned from her own tea party and Dominic suggested that Cressida should take him down to see the church and discuss the plans for the wedding. She immediately invited Julia to go with them.

But this time Julia let her down, because the girl had to go home and reluctantly left her friend and the attractive Dominic.

Cressida had no excuse now for *not* being alone with Dominic. So he took her off in the white Mercedes. They drove to St. Albans, and entered the church by a side door.

The Vicar happened at that moment to be there. He stopped to speak to Cressida and was introduced to Dominic.

"Very important job for you—the Best Man has quite a responsibility," he smiled.

"It will be my first experience," Dominic smiled back, shaking the Vicar's hand. "Let's hope I don't drop the ring. The bridegroom told me yesterday that I have to keep it until such time as you ask for it."

"Quite, quite," murmured the Vicar. The Reverend Edmund Sykes was a tall, pale young man with glasses and rather large ears. With his long nose and mild brown eyes, he struck Dominic as looking exactly like a spaniel. His fingers suddenly ached to draw a cartoon of the reverend gentleman which fact he whispered in Cressida's ear after they left him and they advanced further into the dim, cool atmosphere of the church.

"Don't make jokes in church," she whispered back.

He continued, trying to shock her. She had certainly changed, he thought. If she wasn't careful she would turn into a little prig.

"Don't you think that the Lord Himself enjoyed the odd joke in His time?"

Cressida frowned and shook her head.

"I suppose so, but one never somehow ties up the thought of the Lord with jokes."

"Maybe there would be more religion and larger congregations if it wasn't all so pompous and *un*funny," said Dominic.

How like him, Cressida thought, to want to be amusing at the wrong moments. He had always had a bitter edge to his tongue and she was convinced he had no place in this little church and was not really the ideal Best Man for Sam, either. Vaguely she remembered that Dominic had once told her he had been brought up as a Catholic, like his mother, but had not attended any church services since he came of age.

Hurriedly she began to discuss the ceremony that would take place on Saturday.

"Just before the wedding begins, you'll go with Sam up into the top right-hand pew, then when I start to come up the aisle on my uncle's arm, you two stand up there—" she pointed to the chancel step. "Then, as the Vicar says, you hand him the ring when he asks for it. I expect Sam's briefed you about seeing that we get into our car, and get to the airport in time and all that," she ended lamely.

"I shall play the part perfectly," said Dominic.

"If you don't mind—" she said a little stiffly and slipped into one of the pews and knelt a moment with her face in her hands.

He did not kneel with her but stood staring at the bowed lovely young head. Somehow the nape of her neck—he could just see the faint circle dividing the sunburn from the whiteness of her skin—gave him a feeling of real affection and even pity. He had always thought Cressida's swan neck beautiful and curiously defenceless. He had sketched it so many times. Now—he felt almost ashamed of standing in this sacred place, conscious that he was still in love with her. In love in Dominic Miln's peculiar, egotistical fashion.

Of course he knew that she was going to belong to Sam in a few days' time and that she would be lost to *him*, and he knew how deeply Sam loved Cressida. The old boy hadn't disguised that fact when he talked about her. But Dominic wondered just how much Cressida *really* returned Sam's absolute love. How much had there been of rebound about this affair, on her part? When he remembered her 'absolute love' for him, he had a sudden crazy desire to snatch her up, take her out of this church and drive off in the Mercedes to the airport—not to Majorca for her honeymoon—to Rome. Back to the old studio. Back to the old crazy, carefree artist's life he had led with her. It had no connection whatsoever with all this pomp and ceremony, all these trappings of a conventional wedding.

Suddenly he bent over her and touched her shoulder.

"Let's get out of here," he whispered roughly.

She turned and looked up at him. The expression in his eyes horrified her although she couldn't begin to analyse it. She only knew that it made her go quite cold, took her breath away.

She walked out of the church with Dominic into the sunlight breathing not very evenly.

"Well—" Dominic was the first to speak, "I presume you've got it all taped. I'm sure it will be what is known as a very pretty wedding and you'll make a very pretty bride. I can see it in print: 'The bride wore white (whatever the material is) with a filmy veil and a virginal crown of orange blossoms. The hands holding the bouquet shook a little, making the stephanotis quiver.' M'm—yes and I presume the bride will be quivering, too . . ."

"Oh, shut up," she swung round on him, her teeth clenched, "shut up, Dominic. How can you be so—*so contemptible?*"

He searched in his pockets for cigarettes and matches and shook the box at her, laughing:

"There's no need to get all het up. I was only joking."

"Just as you joked as we went into the church. You have an extraordinary sense of humour!" she said, and marched towards the car—hating him—hating her memories —hating the fate that had brought him back into her life. It was too unkind a jest, she thought, and the tears gushed into her eyes and blinded her for a second. Dominic saw her wipe the tear away with the back of her hand. Immediately he was all contrition. He came to her side:

"I'm sorry, Little Cat. I do apologise. It was perfectly beastly of me. I can only excuse myself by saying that when I saw you kneeling there, praying, it had the most devastating effect on me. I just couldn't stand it somehow."

"Why not?" she swung round and the green eyes blazed up at him. In the middle of the battle of words between them, the artist in him was ravished by the beauty of those blazing eyes. He wished he could put that colour, that light, on to canvas. She said:

"First of all, please stop calling me *Little Cat*. You've *got* to stop it. I don't like it any more, and if Sam ever hears it will make him wonder—Oh God—don't you understand?"

"Oh Sam," muttered Dominic, "*Sam!*"

"Yes, and you needn't say his name like that. You've already admitted that he's a wonderful person and that he's not got to be hurt."

"All right, calm down, my sweet. I'm not going to hurt him.

He holds all the trump cards, anyhow. You're going to marry him, aren't you? I don't really count."

"No, you don't, why should you?" she flashed, near to tears again.

She could not bear this storm that was raging around and inside her. The idea that Dominic still had it in his power to create havoc in her was so unnerving.

She wished he had never come down to Brighton. She wished she had not taken him to the church. She wished she had never met or loved him. But she had wished those things so many times, and what was the use? What could you ever gain out of looking back and wishing that things had been different? It was all too futile.

One thing she did know; when he had made those jokes about the local press review of the wedding, all her joy, the tranquillity of spirit which had been Sam's gifts to her, had vanished. Now she felt utterly demoralised. It struck her with alarming force that she had no right to wear what Dominic had called a virginal crown, and no right to the white veil which for centuries had been worn by the bride to hide her from the eyes of others. A symbolic veil that should be lifted only for *him*.

Was all *that* silly and outdated? Just tradition to be lightly accepted and followed? Wasn't it hypocritical? Didn't thousands of weddings take place (and would take place in the future) with a bride who had no right to either crown or veil? Was it all just a matter to be skimmed over and conveniently forgotten? Were churches these days only places in which people went to attend weddings, baptisms and funerals, and not very often to pray?

Cressida became conscious in these few moments of a dreadful confusion of ideas, principles and ethics that she could not begin to sort out. Certainly not with *this man* standing beside her, looking at her with those strange dark magnetic eyes of his—eyes which had once had such power to move her and control her emotions.

She made a frantic effort to lift herself out of the waters that were threatening to close over her head.

"Let's get this clear, Dominic. I love Sam and I'm going

to marry him and nothing that you can do or say will alter it."

"Cressida, darling—you misjudge me—I haven't come here with any such intention—" began Dominic.

"Well, you shouldn't keep alluding to what's past and done with," she broke in, "it's not only beastly but wrong of you."

He looked down into the stormy young face and now suddenly he smiled with real tenderness.

"Forgive me, Cressida. I hate myself. But I still happen to be very fond of you."

"Well, I'm not fond of you," she declared childishly.

Dominic was not prepared to accept that statement, but he let it pass.

"Come on, get into the car—I'll take you somewhere for a drink. Let's stop being quite so melodramatic," he said.

"No, thank you. I'd like to go home."

"Darling, I've come a long way—won't you let me spend an hour or two with you? I promise to be good. We'll just talk about art or Sam—or the island of Majorca—anything you like except ourselves."

"No, thanks. I'd rather go home."

"Are you determined to dislike me?"

"Yes," she said and meant it.

"I'm sorry," he said and shrugged his shoulders. He added that maybe she would feel more kindly about him when she got back from her honeymoon.

"You shouldn't take me or anything that I say so seriously," he ended. "You ought to know me by now. I've never been conventional and I didn't think you were. I suppose you've changed."

"Yes," she said and put a handkerchief against her lips and pressed it tightly as she got into the Mercedes beside him. She was calming down and beginning to regret that she had ever allowed herself to be so disturbed.

As they drove off, Dominic said:

"I certainly seem to have put my foot into it. Stupid of me. I didn't mean it."

No, she thought, I don't suppose you meant to do what you did in Rome, but you did it.

"On the other hand," he went on, "it's all a bit awkward

for me. Sam is so anxious for me to officiate at this wedding."

Even as he said the words, he asked himself why he was worrying about what *Sam* wanted. Perhaps Cressida was right. He had an odd sense of humour—almost a perverted one—and he did find it rather an ironic and amusing situation. The bride, the first lover and the husband—all together at the altar steps.

Of course, he knew he ought to go away this moment and never see Cressida again. But that would have been the right thing and Dominic had never been noted for doing what was right. Suddenly he said:

"Were you interested in that sale at Christie's when the Rembrandt fetched all that money and went to America instead of to Lord Somerset?"

There was the old Dominic again, she thought. He had the sort of brain that swung from idea to idea with startling rapidity. He never fastened on any one topic of conversation and held on to it. She honestly believed that Dominic's mind was rather like his passions—brilliant but fragmentary—changing, circling, dipping like swallows in flight. That had been one of his fascinations and he never seemed conscious of the effect it sometimes had on more simple-minded people. Here he was talking about the sale of paintings while she was still shaking with a sense of acute mental disturbance. It only showed how little anything really meant to him—except art, and on that subject, of course, he was solid and very serious indeed.

They discussed the sale of the Rembrandt, which she remembered seeing in the papers and reading aloud to her father. Soon they entered into one of their old discussions. She had never, of course, been able to keep up to Dominic's level, but it hadn't mattered *then*. It would end in her making some frightful mistake and being gathered into his arms, and between kisses he would whisper:

"My silly, ignorant Little Cat. Your lips are like velvet. You don't have to *know* things. You just have to look like you do, and be what you are—a sweet, foolish adorable cat."

"Oh Sam," she whispered to herself. "Sam, I wish you

were here and that I could hang on to you just for a moment and get rid of this devil that's pursuing me!"

But she was herself again by the time they reached the bungalow. She and Dominic had had their argument; she expressed the regret that the best paintings and, indeed, the best of so many treasures—were all going out of the country. He said, what did it matter? As long as the treasures could be seen in some museum and appreciated by the world at large, who cared where the museum was? The only thing he deplored was when some uneducated millionaire bought a masterpiece because he thought it was the thing to do and might just as well have hung a cheap coloured photograph over his fireplace.

The big Mercedes came to a standstill. Dominic turned to Cressida:

"I'm sorry you won't come down to Brighton and have a drink and some food with me. I'll promise to remain completely impersonal, if you'll change your mind."

"I'd rather not," she said stiffly.

He looked at her with admiration.

"You've gained poise, haven't you? You're much more determined than you used to be too."

"Just as well."

"Oh, Cressida—don't be cynical—it doesn't suit you, darling. Sorry—I know I mustn't call you *darling*. I really must behave. I *will* if you'll just be a little more friendly—not so intense about everything."

She flushed and stepped out of the car.

Perhaps she *was* being too intense, she thought. Perhaps she just wasn't like some girls who could remain impersonal and unmoved in the presence of a man they had once loved and given the world to. Perhaps she would be doing Sam more of a service, too, if she behaved as Dominic did—without conscience.

She made an effort to relax, smiled and held out a hand.

"Good-bye, Dominic. I'm afraid I'm a bit on edge—I think I might be excused for it—after all a wedding is a very serious affair. I don't believe you meant to upset me. It's just *you*."

"That's it, darling. It's just me," he grinned, "and I want very much to cement my friendship with you and Sam when you get back to England again. You know I'm going to be working in London for the rest of this summer and autumn and I do want you, in particular, to see some of my sets for the opera. I'd like your opinion."

She felt strangely compelled to stay and talk to Dominic. He was being suddenly voluble about his newly-formed association with Canletti. He and Aldo got on very well, he said, and it was a pity that Cressida hadn't been at the first night of La Tosca in Milan. When the curtain went up, there had been an ovation lasting for several minutes because of his, Dominic's, cathedral set.

Once again Cressida was caught up in the fascination of listening to Dominic—fascinated—mildly amused by his vanity, his immense belief in himself—that slightly *un*English way he had of boasting instead of understating his own talents, as Sam would have done. How charming he was! Devilishly so.

She tried not to feel friendly, but there was one thing she had never been able to resist—that was when Dominic had treated her as an equal, despite her ignorance, and asked her opinion about his own work. He used to tell her that she had a natural flair for colour and design. He was asking her now to take an interest in his job.

"Aren't you glad I've got one? You once told me not to be so lazy," he smiled at her.

"I think it sounds marvellous," she said.

"Does Sam like pictures?"

She hesitated. When it came to the question of choosing a painting for their home, Sam hadn't a clue. He left it all to her. But loyally she said:

"Oh, I think Sam's very appreciative and his stepfather— Sir Guy Fennell—has one or two fine portraits in his home which I am sure Sam will take you to see."

"Sam's already told me I've got to draw the famous Franny."

"I'm sure you could do a wonderful painting of her. She's very striking."

Dominic looked at her thoughtfully.

"Oh, well," he said, "I think I had better push off. Do you think it would be nice if I contacted your little blonde friend, Julia, and took her out to dinner? The Best Man ought to be on good terms with the Chief Bridesmaid."

That floored Cressida. She was positive that she didn't feel any jealousy because that would have been absurd but for all kinds of reasons, she didn't want Dominic to start anything with young Julia who had already been roused to interest in the attractive Best Man.

Betty Chalmers wouldn't thank her for encouraging anything but the most casual acquaintanceship between her teenage sister-in-law and Dominic Miln—Cressida was sure of that.

A few moments ago she had been thinking that she had misjudged him and that all the nonsense he talked was just on the surface; that he had never meant to be deliberately cruel to her either, nor guessed how atrociously she had suffered through him. Perhaps if she went on feeling resentment and hatred towards him—and kept trying to put him right out of her life—Sam would suspect that something was wrong. It would make everything much more difficult for them all. More than ever, she was confident that Sam must never guess at the truth about Dominic and herself.

"Can you give me young Julia's telephone number?" she heard Dominic ask her.

"By all means," she said rather coldly, and gave it. "But please, Dominic, don't—"

"Don't what?"

She read a cynical amusement in those dark, narrow eyes of his and for no reason at all the colour burnt her cheeks. He added:

"Are you afraid I'll try and start something with that child?"

She felt too embarrassed to answer. He laughed and said in a low voice:

"Cressida, my pet, you've always taken me too seriously. Don't forget that I am half a Latin. I think I'm more realistic about sex than you are. Love should be splendid, but if it's taken too seriously it can become tragic, you know."

She did know, but she wasn't going to admit it and turned her burning face from him.

"I haven't the least idea what you are talking about," she said. "I must go—good-bye until Saturday and thank you again for coming down to see me."

He drove off, still smiling. He left her standing there feeling cold in the sunshine. She knew today—as she had known six months ago in Rome—that she was quite incapable of coping with Dominic. She was too impulsive and transparent. He always saw through her, and because he had no scruples he could not be made to feel that it was ever he who was in the wrong.

It was positively maddening.

When she met Freda in the hall and her mother started to say what a charming man Mr. Miln was, Cressida snapped:

"You're so easily charmed, Mummy."

Then she marched into her own bedroom. Freda stared after her open-mouthed. Dear, *dear*, she thought, Cressie was in one of her moods again. Poor darling . . . It was her privilege to have 'nerves' just before the wedding. But Freda was a little troubled because John had asked her just now, as she wheeled him indoors, if she didn't think it a bit odd that Cress had never mentioned Mr. Miln's name to them before. Yet she seemed to have known him quite well out in Rome.

Could it be that Cress and this artist . . . but no . . . Freda's imagination carried her no further. Mr. Miln was a friend of Sam rather than Cressida. To think along other lines would be what Cressida would call 'Mummy's romancing'. Cressida spent the next half an hour having a bath and changing her dress and endeavouring to drive the 'blackout' as Sam called it, away. She succeeded and finally appeared in the kitchen to help her mother get the evening meal. She was cool and cheerful again. She had thrown off all the feeling of anger and confusion into which Dominic's visit had thrown her. She told herself that she wasn't even going to care whether Dominic took Julia out in Brighton tonight or not, but she was going to make quite sure that she warned the young girl against him. That would be her duty.

"I'm beginning to feel an old married woman before I'm married," she told herself with some amusement.

She telephoned the Chief Bridesmaid next morning. To her relief Julia made it quite clear that she had *not* gone out with Dominic Miln last night. She told Cressida that she had been to a party given by Betty, her sister-in-law, and met rather a nice boy there. At the same time, she added:

"But I say, Cress, darling, I'm simply mad about Sam's Best Man. I think he's smashing."

"Well, don't lose a night's sleep over *him*," Cressida warned her grimly, "he's frightful with girls—you just want to be careful."

"You sound like Mummy," laughed Julia.

Yes, thought Cressida . . . here she was aged twenty-three and beginning to think and talk like her own mother. Full of warnings to teenagers! And what good had Mummy's training ever done *her*? It had only led her down the very path of wild romance, towards an even wilder regret.

7

It was generally accepted in the Rayes' circle that Cressida's wedding was one of the most delightful there had ever been in the little Church of St. Albans.

It was a brilliant summer's day. Cressida could not have asked for better weather and she had been rather anxious the day before when it had rained without stopping. But on her wedding morning the sun broke through. By the time she left for the church with Uncle Bill, it was fine and warm. The bright rim of the sea glittered like a line of blue-green glass against the horizon.

The church was not too full because Cressida and Sam had agreed that it should be a small wedding. The organist played beautifully and the Rev. Edmund Sykes had a nice voice and delivered his words sympathetically rather than with the dull, nasal intoning of so many in his calling.

Cressida had passed through a few moments of blind panic as she stood before the long mirror in her mother's bedroom, and Freda and the two bridesmaids hovered around, arranging her train and the long floating veil.

Always pale, she had put on just a little rouge today, and darkened her lashes. She knew—they told her so—that she looked beautiful. As all brides should look—her very best. Slim and graceful in the lovely flowing dress with the long tight sleeves and boat-shaped neck. She wore one beautiful brooch —rubies and diamonds to match her engagement ring—set like a cluster of red flowers with diamond petals on delicate gold stems. Franny's choice, and Sam's wedding present to Cressida.

Franny, herself, had given her a really handsome present— a mink stole of a delicate shade of pale golden-brown. The first real fur Cressida had ever owned. She was enraptured with it, and it was ready if she wanted it, although owing to the brilliance of the day she ought not to need it.

When they put the bouquet of yellow roses into her hands,

the long green fronds of stephanotis trailed down to her knees and she could not help remembering Dominic's cruelly sarcastic words:

"The hands holding the bouquet shook a little . . . and I presume the bride will be quivering, too."

She was haunted by the memory of that cruel and too apt prophecy. Her hands *were* quivering and the stephanotis *did* shake. Her throat felt dry although her eyes were hard and bright.

She wasn't going to be hysterical and silly, she decided. She had quite made up her mind to disassociate herself completely from the past. But she did wish Dominic wasn't going to be there at the church, with Sam.

She turned and looked at her mother who gazed back at her, her round, pink face transfigured with love.

"You look heavenly, my darling . . .!"

"Heavenly," echoed the two bridesmaids.

Julia, herself, looked very attractive. The almond green dress suited her gold and white prettiness. Cousin Victoria was no beauty, but she, too, looked fresh and sweet, with the plump figure of youth, a head of curly fair hair, and a face that radiated good humour. Both girls were excited and chattered like two magpies. Simon Raye hovered in the background. Simon was scrubbed and polished up for the occasion. He had smarmed his usually wild mop of fair hair down with a brand of oil which the family deplored. It had such a strong odour. But Freda had seen to it that the young boy's dark suit had been well pressed. Daddy was downstairs in his chair—waiting for them—spruced up for the occasion. He had insisted upon struggling into his old morning-coat, now too big for his gaunt frame, and Cressida has picked a yellow rosebud from her own bouquet to put in his buttonhole. Uncle Bill was waiting with him—ready to escort the bride.

Simon grinned at his sister's reflection in the mirror.

"I say, you do look smashing, Cress. I've got the ink bottle all ready to throw."

"You do it and Sam will beat you," she smiled back.

"Good old Sam! Fancy taking *you* on—" began Simon derisively, but was checked by his mother.

"That's enough, scallywag. You treat the bride with respect and remember that in a very few moments she will be Mrs. R. S. Paull and you can't go talking to a married woman as though she were one of your school buddies."

"We don't have girls in our school," said Simon, "they're too soppy."

Everybody laughed including the bride who suddenly felt better and stopped shaking. The family were so sweet—so good to her. Her parents especially so, scraping up every penny possible for this great day.

A striped blue and white marquee had been put up in the garden yesterday. The caterers were busy at this moment arranging food and champagne.

Cressida thought how marvellous Sam had been (as usual). Knowing his future father-in-law's financial position, with Simon still to educate, Sam had insisted upon supplying the champagne himself. After all, there were going to be over a hundred people, small though the wedding was. Champagne was not cheap.

At least half of the guests were friends of Sam's and his mother, too, and a few of Guy Fennell's among them.

When the moment came for Cressida to walk up the aisle on her uncle's arm, she felt quite cool and poised. She had fought down her nerves. She was able to look, without a tremor, at the two young men standing by the chancel step. There they were—the tall, broad-shouldered one with the white carnation in his buttonhole who was her bridegroom—her Sam; Sam whom she was sure now that she loved as much as he loved her. There was Dominic, a little shorter and slimmer, with his arresting face and restless hands. The one watching her approach, blue eyes full of adoration. The other one admiring her too, but with a slight ironic lift of brows and lips.

She ignored Dominic completely.

She looked only at Sam then at the priest standing in front of her as he began with the opening words of the Marriage Service.

"Dearly beloved, we are gathered together . . ."

After that everything seemed to go quickly and smoothly.

Later, Cressida told herself that she had really felt like somebody in a dream. Her feet weren't planted firmly on the ground, although she made all the responses so clearly that her friends told her afterwards they had heard every word.

It was a wonderful comforting moment for her when Sam took her left hand and held it so tightly that it almost hurt. She needed that warmth and strength. She would always need it, she thought. Everything was going to be all right. She didn't feel a hypocrite or a sinner today. Whatever she had done in the past, God forgave repentant sinners—that was what the Bible taught, anyhow, and she could begin again and from now onwards she would be faithful to Sam, and live only for him.

She was no longer aware of Dominic's presence. And if he was looking her way, she didn't care. She didn't care what he was thinking, either. She was barely conscious of the fact that he gave the ring to Sam, but as Sam slipped it on to her finger, she looked straight up into those very blue eyes of his and felt strangely triumphant. He was a wonderful person and his love would shield her. The past could not touch her. She had nothing more to fear.

She heard the solemn words from the Vicar:

"Whom God hath joined together let no man put asunder."

No man will, she thought, no one on earth will part Sam and myself.

Behind her, during the prayers that followed, Freda Raye shed a few tears. In his wheelchair in the aisle, Dr. Raye wiped his own eyes, but was happy and thankful that his beloved daughter had married such a splendid boy. Simon, too young to understand the solemnity of the church ceremony, grinned to himself, wishing that he could indeed carry out his awful threat to throw ink over his sister's bridal dress. Although, of course, it was only a joke. He wouldn't *dream* of doing such a thing. He was jolly fond of old Cress, and Sam was a smasher. Best Three-quarter they'd ever had in the Cambridge Rugger team in Sam's time. Simon was blissful at the thought that he would be taken in future to all the International Matches and sit in a seat of honour with his brother-in-law. The other chaps at school were jolly envious.

On the bridegroom's side of the church, Lady Fennell stood looking at her tall, fair son and the girl who was now his wife, her feelings mixed. She was reminded perhaps of her own church wedding to Sam's father twenty-seven years ago—longer than Franny cared to remember—and of the vows she had taken and often regretted. Martin had been a darling, but not really her type and she hadn't been cut out to be a good, little housewife who needed to economise. Neither had motherhood suited her. Guy didn't suit her either, of course, he was far too intellectual, and he bored her to tears. But his cheque-book was ample compensation and it was a good thing really that Sam would now live in a home of his own. She didn't really want a grown man of his age hanging around the place. Without him she could *really* go back to being called old Guy Fennell's *young* wife.

She had to admit that Cressida looked really beautiful—physically much more so than Diana, for instance. And the Rayes were all very sweet people, but so *ordinary*. Such a pity darling Sam couldn't have done better for himself. Also—Franny squirmed a little at the idea—that it mightn't be long now before the young couple presented her with a grandchild.

It was all very well people saying that it didn't matter and and that there were so many glamorous grannies these days. Franny couldn't *bear* the prospect. It spoiled her fun. At the same time, she knew that she looked wonderful and really youthful today in her exquisite off-white suit (made by Balmain) and the huge black and white hat with a turned back brim, also especially made for her by Simone Mirman. Of course, she was the smartest woman in the church. She always liked to be *that*, wherever she went, and thank goodness, she had got Sam to ask Sir Colin and Lady Ryvingdon to the wedding. Meryl Ryvingdon was Sam's godmother but out of deference to Franny's feelings, never publicly broadcast the fact because Meryl, like Franny, looked twenty years younger than she really was; and Colin who had lately been Governor of a colony which no longer had a white government, had just been given a very important post in England. They added 'tone' to the party. Besides which, Meryl had almost persuaded Franny that Cressida was so beautiful and such an unusual sort of girl, Franny should be thankful. She might have had a much worse daughter-in-law.

Too true, Franny decided, remembering that the son of one of her friends had just married a shopgirl whose people were the *bottom*.

At least Sam's father-in-law was a *doctor*.

The wedding was over. The organ swelled softly. Franny and Guy followed the Rayes into the vestry where the bride and bridegroom must sign the registry.

Franny embraced first her son and then her new daughter-in-law.

"*Dahling!*" she said with theatrical fervour, "You have *all* my good wishes and you look divine."

"Thank you so much, Franny," said Cressida. Her cheek had a pink flush now which was not all rouge, and her eyes were starry.

"My goodness, I've got me a devastatingly beautiful wife," said Sam in a low, awed voice.

Dominic moved forward:

"Best Man's privilege," he said smoothly, took Cressida's hand and, bending, kissed her on both cheeks.

Just for an instant the light went out of Cressida's eyes. She couldn't *bear* those two kisses. Perhaps it was dramatising the position, but she really could have whispered the word '*Judas*' as he bent down. Yet his fingers held hers very lightly and his lips barely touched her cheeks. Then he moved back again. But he had looked straight down into her eyes and she hadn't liked what she saw in them. He *couldn't mustn't* look at her like that with such poignant intimacy. It was outrageous of him.

She turned away, her heart galloping, and grabbed at Sam's arm.

"My husband," she said in a clear rather defiant voice.

Speechlessly, Sam pressed her arm to his side. He had fought hard to get this girl and he felt humble as well as victorious now that he had got her. Incredible to think that Cressida was his wife. When he had seen her walking up the aisle in all her bridal beauty, he had thought that he had never seen anything so lovely. As for old Dom, he had done Tim's job splendidly.

But there was still a lot to be done before he could take his wife off, away from the maddening crowd, to the solitude they both longed for, and Sam knew it.

He hugged and kissed dear Freda, shook hands with the doctor and his new uncle, William Raye, whom he thought a very nice fellow indeed—a bit like the doctor, only younger-looking, without so much grey in his hair, and wearing horn-rimmed spectacles.

As they returned to the church and the organ broke into the triumphant strains of Mendelssohn's Wedding March, Dominic followed with the bridesmaids, thinking his own deep and rather uncomfortable thoughts.

He wasn't the type to be discomfited or embarrassed by much in life. Not he, with his rather cold cynical appraisal of society and human beings in general. But the artist in him was always moved by beauty and he, too, had thought he had never seen anything lovelier than Cressida during the wedding. He had made mock of the veil and the coronet of flowers—he had tried to satirise the whole show. Yet he had to admit there was something moving about it all, and when he had touched the perfumed velvet of Cressida's cheek and remembered those other mad exciting kisses, he hadn't felt too happy. He had thought himself invulnerable, yet wondered now if he really was. He also began to wonder seriously whether he had not allowed something very beautiful and perfect to slip out of his hands—into Sam Paull's. It could be lonely being a bachelor even one like himself with money and interesting work. Promiscuity had its drawbacks. There had been many women before Cressida and one in Rio afterwards—a dazzling little brunette whom he had painted and who had been mad about him. But the memory of Cressida had somehow continued to haunt Dominic, and he had found himself quoting Swinburne:

"*The bitterness of things too sweet . . . The broken singing of the dove . . .*

Cressida's love—Cressida herself had been too sweet at

93

times and it was he who with a ruthless shot, had wounded the dove. At the time he hadn't suffered from more than a brief period of regret and wanting her back. But he had learned that she could not be put right out of mind like the others. Sam had called her a 'unique' girl; Dominic had to agree. Unique Cressida was, with a peculiar attraction. Creature of moods, yes; moved as easily to tears as laughter . . . swift to learn, to understand and appreciate. Swift to respond. How madly he had loved her during those brief few weeks in Rome. And now all that beauty—that curious innocence that she had never really lost—would be Sam's.

Dominic felt a sudden distaste for being here at the wedding and wished he could clear out of it, but, of course, he had to stay on and do his job until the end.

When pretty Julia with her golden hair and Greuze face whispered something to him about the bride looking a dream, he threw off his depression and flirted with her.

"Ah! But think what a beautiful bride *you'd* make with that blonde hair shining through the veil. I've a good mind to rush out, get a Special Licence and drag *you* to the altar myself, young Julia."

She giggled and blushed.

"Oh, you are *awful*!"

Delightedly she continued the flirtation, but Dominic hardly heard what she whispered to him.

Half-heartedly he took his place in the wedding group which had to be photographed outside the church door where a little crowd waited with confetti. At last he broke away from them all and made it his business to find the big car that had been hired to take the bride and groom back to the reception.

Once the bride and bridegroom had driven off, Dominic dutifully carried out the rest of his tasks feeling that he had never needed a drink more and slightly anguished because he couldn't turn tail and run. God, what a fool he had been ever to embark on this affair; but when he had first promised Sam, he hadn't, of course, realised that the bride would be Cressida.

The reception was as sucessful as the wedding.

Cressida stood beside her tall husband just inside the open flap of the marquee 'receiving'. The guests trailed past. Kisses and congratulations and good wishes were exchanged. Now everybody was in festive mood and there was popping of corks, a hum of voices, and gradually the marquee was filled with gaily-dressed women in summery hats. Some strolled out in the sunshine.

Freda felt proud and pleased, standing by her husband's chair, shaking hands with everybody. Sir Guy and Lady Fennell stood beside her. Franny was relaxed and happy now because so many people she hadn't met before murmured that it was *impossible* that she should be the bridegroom's mother—she looked like his *sister*.

Dominic no longer went anywhere near Cressida. He felt remote and sullen—quite unlike himself. Only with difficulty he continued his futile flirtation with pretty Julia whose blue eyes were becoming altogether too melting and inviting to suit him. He was glad when finally he managed to detach himself from Julia and her friends and got into a corner with Guy Fennell whom he thought a rather pleasant old man. He knew something about painting. They had that in common. Dominic also privately considered Guy Fennell too nice to be married to what he called that 'ghastly woman' Franny. If there was one type Dominic couldn't stand, it was the middle-aged woman who dreaded the passing of time and lined herself up with the young girls, using every artifice and trick a beautician could offer. Another few years and Franny would be paying three figures to have her face lifted, he thought.

Cressida hardly saw Dominic to speak to during the reception. She actually found herself looking around, wondering what had happened to him, as time went on. He was conspicuous by his absence.

Then, she and Sam cut the cake, Uncle Bill made a speech, Daddy also said a few words from his chair and Sam replied, making everybody laugh with a few very amusing and well-chosen words. Then Dominic was forced into the scene again. It was the Best Man's duty to propose the toast to the bridesmaids.

Dominic spoke briefly but glibly. As the guests applauded, he looked towards the bride and caught her eye. Then he walked straight up to her.

"It's been a lovely wedding. I congratulate you both," he said very stiffly, "but do you think it would put the cat among the pigeons if I departed before the end? I know I ought to see you off, but I've suddenly developed one of my bad migraines. I'm practically blind with pain. I'm afraid I'll have to let you down."

Sam was at once concerned.

"Oh, I say, Dom, I'm awfully sorry—" he began.

"You will understand and excuse me, won't you?" cut in Dominic.

"Of course, but we're awfully sorry, aren't we, darling?" Sam turned to Cressida.

"Yes, very," she said.

She felt her lashes fluttering nervously. That look in Dominic's eye—it was there again—troubling her. That deep, dark, brooding look which used to devastate her so utterly. *Why* did he have to go on looking at her that way? Why had he suddenly got this bad headache? In all the time she had known him, she had never heard Dominic complain of *migraine*. She felt sure it was an idle excuse. Either he was genuinely bored and couldn't stand the party a moment longer, or he had a more personal and hidden reason for quitting.

Dominic said:

"I'll ask that tall usher boy—I think his name is Mitchell —to see you safely off. You'll be at the Savoy tonight, won't you? You fly to Majorca in the morning. You've got your tickets and everything?"

"Yes, everything," said Sam, "you don't have to worry. Rotten thing, migraine. They can be hell. Franny used to get them."

Franny at this moment bore down upon the bridal pair and beckoned to Sam.

"Come here a moment, will you dear? I want you to talk to Colin Ryvingdon," and she added in a low, confidential voice. "He wants a new stockbroker, Meryl says, here's your chance!"

"What—business on my wedding day? Really, Franny!" Sam protested, laughing, but his mother took his arm and pulled him towards Sir Colin. If one could make money, one should do so whatever the time or place—in her estimation.

Cressida faced Dominic. Just for a few seconds they were quite alone in that crowd. Cressida's fingers plucked nervously at her long veil. Then she pulled her dress into a swirl about her feet. Her heart was thumping with rather unpleasant speed. She said:

"I'm really very sorry about your migraine, Dominic. I didn't know you suffered from them."

"I don't. But I need to give some good excuse for leaving."

"I'm sorry it's been so boring for you—" she began.

He interrupted:

"You know it isn't that. Weddings are always boring, but actually I bit off more than I can chew when I agreed to act this part of Best Man before I realised that you were the bride. I've found it singularly unattractive, if you want to know."

That floored her. She really didn't know what to say. It was too embarrassing. The last thing she wanted was for Dominic to behave this way and it seemed so unlike him. She knew that he had always prided himself on being devoid of normal stereotype feelings and personal emotions—except where art was concerned. He could be deeply, almost unbearably moved, by a masterpiece, but, as he had told her, he never allowed himself to get into the stupid, sentimental state that was normally expected of a man in love. He didn't fall in love like other men. For a period of time he could be absorbed in one particular woman (as he had done in her case) but wanting her—appropriating her time—those things were different from being in love in the selfless way Sam loved, for instance. He, Dominic, would never allow himself to be totally governed by his passions, nor had he ever suffered from a conscience. What, then, was the matter with him today, Cressida wondered? Why should he feel that he had 'bitten off more than he could chew'? The very idea startled her because it suggested that her marriage to Sam had upset him. It didn't make sense, Cressida thought resentfully. Dominic was managing to project his personality and his particular feelings into this great moment of her life, and it was monstrous of him. She stared at him, speechlessly.

Dominic suddenly took her hand—the one with the new

shining ring—looked at it and then dropped it. His mouth had taken a bitter downward curve.

"Oh, well—felicitations. I shall think of you two lovers wandering through the flower-filled gardens of The Formentor, gazing enraptured into the sea—soaked by the sun, etc., etc."

Cressida, forgetting that he was supposed to have a headache, said furiously:

"How hateful of you to be so sarcastic. Are you trying to spoil my wedding day?"

"Could I?" he asked meaningly.

She tossed her head, crimson-cheeked, stormy-eyed.

"Oh, go away—do—I think it's better you do," she said.

He shrugged his shoulders and turned away from all that burning beauty that he somehow found on this day of all days to be so much more disturbing than it had seemed in Rome. How freakish, how cynical fate could be. He was positively falling in love for the first time in his life—and with a girl that he might have married, a girl he had run away from and who was now another man's wife.

"Good-bye, Cressida," he said abruptly, "I assure you if I wasn't so tied up with Canletti, I'd fly back to Brazil tomorrow."

She hadn't the least idea why he was suddenly making this scene. She only knew that it was most upsetting; that dearly though she loved the man to whom she had just been married, Dominic was managing to destroy her peace of mind.

"I think it's a pity you *can't* go back to Brazil," she said childishly.

"Why should you care what I do or don't do? It can't possibly affect you, my dear Mrs. Paull," he said, his dark, gloomy eyes looking down at her with derision.

Her new name, coming from his lips, reminded her why she was here in this room, why she was wearing this beautiful bridal dress, and what the whole reception signified. She lashed out at Dominic.

"Please go and don't come and see Sam and me if you can't—if you can't—oh, if *you can't be more sensible!*" she stuttered.

She was rewarded by a loud laugh from Dominic.

"You destroy me, darling, really! You're so exquisitely naïve. Asking me to be sensible. How too ingenuous of you. But don't let's quarrel. If anybody's been a bloody fool, it's me. You've been wise, choosing such a damn good fellow as Sam. You go off with him and be happy and forget me. Sorry I intruded. Good-bye again."

He turned and vanished in the crowd, Cressida stared after him, her face as white now as her bridal gown. It was dreadful, she thought, that she should allow herself to be affected by anything that Dominic Miln said—or did. But certainly his extraordinary behaviour and what he had said just now were not calculated to bring her any pleasure, or bode well for a future friendship between him, and Sam, and herself. She could only try to cool down and put him right out of mind and hope that she would see only a little, if it must be anything, of him in the future.

Her young brother came up to her, grinning from ear to ear.

"Hi, sis. Has your husband quit you already?"

Cressida ruffled her brother's hair, and spoke to him with some relief.

"Hi, Simon! Are you having a good time?"

"Terrific," he said, "I've had six sandwiches, three iced cakes, two ice-creams, three bottles of Coke and now I'm starting on the wedding cake."

"You're a greedy little pig," she murmured.

Sam, having broken away from Franny's friends, came striding back to his bride's side and slipped an arm through hers.

"Darling, you shouldn't be alone. It's Franny's fault—she dragged me away just now. I couldn't stand being parted from my wife. It was *hell*."

"Darling Sam," she pressed his arm tightly to her side and hastily dabbed her lashes because she felt the tears suddenly stinging her eyelids. She added: "I do love you. You're going to be such a marvellous husband."

"Nothing like as marvellous as my Cressida deserves. Where's old Dom? Has he gone?"

"Yes," said Cressida slowly "he's gone."

8

DESPITE the warnings they had been given that Majorca
would be crowded with tourists in the month of August,
Cressida and Sam were glad that they had made it their choice.
They found the island enchanting, and The Formentor one
of the most beautiful hotels in the world.

The white terraces, gay with flowers, sparkled in the sunlight like the blue, blue sea below. There were wonderful
walks everywhere in the green shade of trees. The local
Spaniards were gay, friendly people. Everything seemed to
Cressida perfect; especially the vivid colours; the little
churches; the lovely brown-faced Spanish girls wearing their
black or white lace mantillas when they went to church; the
brown-faced fishermen, and the little cafés where a cosmopo-
litan crowd sat and drank coffee or wine in the sun.

For a greater part of the time, Cressida and Sam got away
from the crowds and wandered off by themselves. They
enjoyed the swimming pool or sitting on the balcony of their
big, luxurious bedroom which faced the sea.

During that fortnight's honeymoon, there was not much
room for regret or memories of Dominic in Cressida's mind.
She gave herself up wholly to the pleasure of being Sam's
wife. She felt relaxed and fulfilled, encircled by his tremendous love and care for her and the unending fervour of his
own happiness; he seemed so immensely proud of her. She was
his heart's desire—and his wife. No girl among all the pretty
girls in Majorca was as beautiful, in Sam's eyes, as his Cressida.

There had been one moment when her joy in this new life,
this ecstasy of being married to a man who loved her so
much was suddenly shattered for an instant. Her happiness
seemed like a beautiful bubble. It can disappear into nothing-
ness with frightening rapidity. Cressida realised that happiness between a man and a woman, no matter how strong or
complete must be safeguarded because of its fragility.

It was on the night of her wedding before they flew to Majorca when they were at the Savoy.

They had had a splendid dinner, and danced every other dance. Sam with his cheek against hers, kept murmuring:

"This is bliss. You really do dance divinely, Mrs. Paull. And you look divine."

Cressida, wearing one of her new trousseau dresses—pleated flowered chiffon with a wide belt which made her waist look incredibly small, and with Sam's ruby and diamond brooch pinned to the bodice—nuzzled her cheek against his and answered:

"I feel divine. I've never been so happy in my whole life."

"Neither have I, darling."

They went on dancing dreamily, whispering a lot of absurd but immensely satisfying things to each other. One or two tired, overdressed and over-made-up women of middle-age looked at the tall, fair young man and the slim dark girl in her flowered chiffon dress with envy. How happy she looked, how young they both seemed. Such a *nice* looking pair!

And to the tired and middle-aged, these two brought a sensation not only of envy but of regret for the past—for the passionate glorious youth that never comes again.

It was while they were drinking their coffee and Sam had lit a cigar and Cressida her cigarette, that her happiness seemed suddenly in peril.

She caught Sam looking at her in that intense way he had when he was being serious and the joking and teasing was over.

"Cressida," he said, "I'll never forget how you looked when you were coming up the aisle. My God, I've been to weddings before and seen some very attractive brides, but *you* were every man's dream."

"You're biased, darling Sam."

"Perhaps. But Dominic thought so too."

"Did he?" said Cressida coolly, and looked at the ash on her cigarette, her brow creased.

"What struck me most," went on Sam, "was that wonderfully remote, inaccessible—sort of look you had on your face. A dedicated sort of expression."

"Quite right. I was about to dedicate my life to you."

"It was more even than a dedication," he persisted, "it was a sort of symbolic expression."

"Symbolic?" she repeated, looking up at him.

"Yes, of your untouched little self. You know what I mean. I realised suddenly what that bridal veil and that coronet really meant. It sort of shook me, darling."

That was the instant when her heart took a downward plunge and the world grew cold. She no longer heard the dance music or was conscious of the people at the tables around them. She no longer even saw Sam's happy, loving face. She stared stonily ahead.

Oh God, she thought, my *untouched little self*—dear, sentimental Sam! He's so very nice. In these days most of the men I've known have seemed more interested in the sensual than the spiritual side of love. Sam's so different!

He was an idealist. She knew that she ought to have told him about Dominic. She knew that she *would have* done so if Dominic hadn't been his great friend. Now she just had to suffer the pangs of conscience in silence.

She wished bitterly that she was harder, less sensitive.

"You look thoughtful, my sweet," said Sam. "Out with it!"

She struggled back into the enchanted hour that had threatened to drift away from her, and stamped a heel hard down on the past.

"What I'm thinking is that my bridegroom looked splendid! I've never seen you in morning rig-out before. It suits you because you're so tall."

Sam raised his champagne goblet to his lips. He laughed.

"Well, I can't say old Dom's fitted *him*. He didn't expect to be asked to such a ceremony so he had to hire a suit. It rather hung on him."

Cressida set her lips then opened them and spoke quite sharply:

"Come and dance again. I like dancing with you."

"That goes for two of us," said Sam happily, and took her out on to the dance floor.

That had been their first dinner-dance together as husband and wife.

Later that night, in his arms, Cressida lay awake while Sam slept with one arm across her. Then only, she cried. Quietly, silently, she was at last reduced to tears. She hardly knew whether because of joy or sorrow. She held one of his hands against her lips while the tears ran down her cheeks. She thought:

I do love you. I'll always be faithful to you. I'll make up for everything that happened in Rome.

In the morning as they laughed and talked over their coffee and rolls, she was happy again. There were no two happier people when they boarded the aircraft for Majorca.

So the lovely sunny days of the honeymoon slid by; all too fast, although Cressida looked forward now to starting life in her little Regency house at home. Theré were, of course, the usual setbacks. Letters arrived from Mummy to say that the electrician doing their work had gone sick and the lights in the lounge were not up; that the decorator had run out of paper, having made an error in his measuring up, so the spare bedroom wouldn't be finished in time. And the Venetian blinds ordered for the kitchen in a special shade of pale blue to match the wallpaper, had not yet arrived. Dear Freda was doing everything she could, but the young couple were in for a few disappointments, she wrote.

Cressida and Sam were much too happy to care.

"It's all in the day's work," said Sam, "and let me tell you no work today is done without something going wrong or somebody letting you down. Franny had the same trouble in London and used to get into a hell of a state every time the men had a tea-break."

"I'm in the hell of a state," said Cressida mischievously, "but not about our house."

He caught her close and laughed and kissed her. They were lying side by side, face downward, by the beautiful swimming pool. They always came here after lunch when there were not many people around. The Spanish hour of 'siesta' took most people indoors.

Sam put an arm across his wife's slim figure. She looked sensational, he thought, in that vivid orange bikini swimsuit with lipstick to match. Like most people with pale skins and dark hair, she had developed a most attractive tan. The graceful legs and arms and straight young back were already a rich gold. She was a lovely thing, he thought, and wondered if any man could be more in love with his wife. He almost felt that he wanted everybody he knew to share in his pride.

They had been here a week now. He had only had one letter from Franny, although he had written twice to her. She didn't mention *them*. She sent two pages about herself—mostly complaining that Guy was getting very mean and that he wouldn't let her change her sapphire mink this autumn for the 'Black Diamond' she wanted to order. Sam had felt slightly annoyed although it took a lot to irritate him; but when he thought how hard money was to make and how many years of economy Cressida had had to practise, and the way that splendid creature, Freda Raye, struggled to make ends meet, he could not be sorry for Franny.

Cressida suddenly remembered a note she had had from her young brother; how she had giggled when she read it aloud to Sam.

"Dear Mrs. Paull (Ha, Ha),
Hope you're having a jolly good honeymoon. It's grim at home as it's been cold and wet ever since you left. You're jolly lucky you've got so much sunshine. Daddy's got a cold. Tell Sam at Lords the other day Middlesex were beaten by Yorkshire. But I don't like cricket as much as Rugger.
Love from Simon."

"I can see that you're going to be Simon's friend for life—with that great Rugger bond between you," Cressida said. "Wasn't his letter funny? Only I didn't like that bit about Daddy having a cold."

"I don't suppose it's anything much—just that beastly change of weather at home."

"I feel rather mean us enjoying all this gorgeous sun with poor Mummy and Daddy and Simon in the rain."

Sam sat up, ran his long fingers through his thick fair hair, and reached in the pocket of the short towelling dressing-jacket beside him for cigarettes.

"That's one of the things I like about you, darling, you think of others and you're so nice to the old folks at home."

She turned on her back and pouted at him as she smoked.

"I wasn't once. I was a beastly selfish girl always occupied with my own thoughts and ideas. I was discontented and restless too, and never appreciated Mummy's Continental kind of affection. I couldn't even bear to be hugged or kissed. I don't know what was wrong with me."

"Just growing up," said Sam, smiling. "I remember being the same at that age. One doesn't know what one wants and then you sort of retire into yourself."

"No, I'm sure you were always nice and you adored Franny who didn't want to adore you. Life is so perverse, Sam."

"Oh, Franny's a law unto herself and so, if it comes to that, are you, my darling."

"Not any more, Sam. I'm a law unto R. S. Paull."

She felt his fingers suddenly caressing the warm nape of her neck.

"It's getting hot out here. Let's go in," he whispered.

She walked with him into the hotel wondering why she had waited so long to say 'yes' to this man; feeling suddenly, light-hearted. She had no interest in anybody else.

But there came another much more difficult moment for her during that otherwise idyllic honeymoon.

It was on their last night in Majorca. They had had a wonderful day. Sam had hired a car and chauffeur to drive them round the island.

"We must do a bit of sightseeing before we leave. We can't just tell them at home that all we really saw was our bedroom and the swimming pool," he had said, grinning at her.

She assured him that she, too, would adore a tour of inspection.

They went to Palma and admired the harbour, but found it too crowded there. They went on to a lovely little place called Colorajada, and across to Puerto Pollensa. Sam knew a man in Calvario who had given up his home in Nairobi and settled in Pollensa with his pretty Viennese wife, and young daughter. They had made a superb house out of a lovely old stone watchtower high on the hill. The Paulls spent a very pleasant hour with them. Cressida, having a Viennese mother, had something in common with the Austrian wife.

When evening came, Sam and Cressida were still not back at The Formentor.

They drove home at a leisured pace and passed through a particularly charming little fishing village which their host in Pollensa had recommended.

Here their car was held up because there were two police cars blocking the narrow village street and quite a crowd milling around. Sam and Cressida got out to see what was happening. There seemed to be a lot of shouting and gesticulating. An elderly woman, with a black veil wound round her head, was screaming and sobbing on the shoulder of a swarthy-faced Mallorcan.

Sam went into a shop, which had the words 'English spoken' in the window.

As he came out, the police drove off so the Paulls were able to get back into their own car and drive on.

Cressida, who felt tired but content, asked if he had found out what all the fuss was about.

"A vendetta, so it would seem," said Sam, "rather a sordid little story."

"What?"

"It appears that there was to have been a wedding today between one of these fishermen fellows and a beautiful young girl named Chiquita. The man in that shop was full of it—all very melodramatic, of course."

"What happened?"

"The bridegroom-to-be discovered, early this morning, that his Chiquita had been palavering with a young visiting salesman from Palma who had fascinated her with his car and his clothes. Only he didn't wish to marry her. The fisherman went mad and killed the wretched girl. The police were doing some further investigating. The tragedy only happened a few hours ago. That was the girl's mother, making all that noise in the street. They have just taken the wretched bridegroom off to gaol. One can't help feeling sorry for him. These Spaniards take this sort of thing very much to heart. They are far more moral in their way than we are. Their girls are usually closely guarded, but Chiquita apparently slipped up."

Sam went on talking as the car moved rapidly down the road back to the Formentor. He had a good memory and could repeat most of the story that the shopkeeper had so eagerly poured into his ears.

Then, suddenly, Sam turned to Cressida, she was looking not at him but straight ahead of her. Her lips were set and her face bore a strained look that puzzled him.

"Have I upset you, darling? I'm afraid it was rather an unhappy tale. Don't let it upset you, please."

She shook her head.

"Give me a cigarette."

"Darling, I've never known you to smoke so much."

She made no comment. After smoking a few seconds, she said:

"Who are you sorriest for—the murderer or the murdered girl?"

"That's rather a fast one. I don't quite know. I'm sorry for them both. These vendettas—of course that's the Italian word, but I don't know what the Spanish one is—don't take place quite so often as they used to," he went on, "I believe they're all getting more modern—even the primitives down here."

"But what I want to know is—do you think he had any right to shoot her?" asked Cressida.

"He actually knifed her. Not so nice," said Sam, grimacing.

Darkness had fallen. The stars were big and bright. They had just left the sea behind them. It had been smooth and bright as silver. It was a wonderful warm Mallorcan night. Usually Cressida found it all so romantic. This evening, romance had given place to realism and of a sinister kind. The significance of what had taken place in that village was hitting her hard. She felt a little sick.

"Come on, Sam," she said. "Tell me—do you think he had any right to kill her?"

"Of course not, darling. There's never any real excuse for a chap taking another person's life. At the same time, one must sympathise with the disappointed bridegroom. Not only disappointed, mark you, but *cheated*."

Oh God, she thought, *Oh God!*

Sam enlarged on the subject.

"It's rather an interesting point, really," added Sam. "After all, she hadn't taken the vows of fidelity. Maybe she meant to be quite faithful to him after the wedding. I don't know how he found out about it. Someone told him, I suppose, but that was really the girl's bad luck. She *might* have got away with it."

Cressida's hands clenched in her lap.

"Yes, that was her bad luck," she said harshly.

"Bad luck for the chap," said Sam lightly. He was quite happy—he felt in no way personally involved in the village tragedy.

But now he took one of his wife's hands and pressed it between his.

"Your hand's very hot, darling. Have you got a temperature. You haven't had too much sun, have you? Let's feel your forehead."

"No, no. I actually feel rather cold."

She gently pushed away his hand.

"Well—don't let's talk about the murder. It's too sad. We don't want sadness. This is the last night of our honeymoon."

She nodded.

But she felt driven to go on discussing the affair. The ghosts of the past were crowding in on her again, clouding her bright vision of happiness. Her conscience began to torture her again. She said, feverishly.

"What would you have done if you were in the young fisherman's shoes and *you* had found that your bride had been sleeping with the salesman from Palma?"

He played with her fingers for a second. She looked up at him through the velvet, purple darkness and saw his eyes shining down at her. She envied him his complete tranquillity.

He answered her gently.

"I really don't know all the answers, dearest. I don't think a man ever knows what he'll do under certain circumstances until he is actually faced with such a crisis."

"Well, you've just intimated that you wouldn't put a knife in her back and well, of course, you wouldn't; you couldn't be brutal enough."

He laughed.

"Darling—it's all a bit too melodramatic. I'm much too Saxon to go in for shootings and knifings out of sex jealousy."

"But how would you *feel* about such a case?" she went on. "I mean if the girl you thought pure as the driven snow turned out to have had a lover and wasn't all that pure."

"Oh, I expect I'd be bloody angry," said Sam in a typically English manner.

"Is that all?"

"Darling—*really*—how you women do love analysis!" laughed Sam. "I don't know *what* I'd do really, sweetie. Certainly I wouldn't feel I could trust her in the same old way, and I'd hate the fact that she had already belonged to someone else, *and* lied to me about it. It would be the deceit I'd dislike rather than what she did in the past with her boyfriend."

Cressida wiped her face with her handkerchief. She suddenly felt that her whole body was damp with perspiration. *So that was how Sam would feel if he knew about Dominic.* He would never trust her again. He'd lose all his present respect for her—his belief—not so much because she had done the wrong thing—but *because she hadn't told him about it.*

Sam added:

"I'm not so pompous and pious that I firmly believe a girl must be 'pure as the driven snow' before marriage. A lot of girls today have their fun and games beforehand. But I happen to be a person with a few ideals and well, I must say I'm very happy to know that my wife was not some other fellow's mistress."

Now it was said.

Cressida, stricken, felt as though dark waters closed over her head and that she literally drowned in them. All the way along, she had been afraid that she had done the wrong thing—now she *knew* it, and it was much too late to tell him, even if she could bring herself to do so, about Dominic.

Oh Sam, she thought, *Sam, I didn't mean to deceive you! If only you hadn't known Dominic—and liked him so much. If only that awful coincidence of him coming back to be our Best Man hadn't happened!*

She shut up like a clam. She had absolutely nothing more to say—no more questions to ask because she had been answered fully. She only knew that because she loved Sam so much, she felt bitterly regretful. She should never have misled him. Even if it had meant hurting him, she should have told him the truth; not let him marry her, believing her to be so perfect. That was where she had gone wrong.

Sam, who had no wish to discuss the tragedy of the fishing village any further, began to talk about their flight home tomorrow. She joined in, feverishly, pretending that all was well. She felt that at any cost to herself she must try to make Sam happy *now*. She owed that to him.

She had never loved him more nor given herself to him more passionately than she did on this their last night in Majorca. Only once she moved away from his embrace and hid her burning face in the pillows. That was when he put his lips against the palm of her hand and said:

"That poor chap they locked up—the one who knifed that girl—God, I feel sorry for him tonight. What a lucky fellow *I am!*"

9

THE honeymoon was over.

The young Paulls came home on one of those dreary August mornings when England looks at her most melancholy —cool and grey, the landscape blurred by a sorry drizzle. It was such a sudden change from the brilliance of Majorca that Cressida felt depressed.

Perhaps, she thought, it was really because this, their first night back, had to be spent in Franny's house. That elegant, luxurious home presided over by Lady Fennell held no charms for Cressida. She was still a little afraid of her mother-in-law— that touch of the vixen under the baby-sweetness. Neither could she ever in her heart forgive Franny for not having made Sam a little happier when he was a child; or for being so selfish and horrid at times to poor old Sir Guy.

However, Cressida knew she and Sam had no choice, because the house in Cowfold was not ready, as they had hoped, to receive them. The electricians had let them down and even the new cooker was not yet installed. Cressida would rather have stayed at the bungalow, but there was not a double room free when Simon was home for the holidays.

Sam had left his Triumph car at the airport garage. He got it only after they were finished with the Customs, then they drove through the light summer rain to London while Cressida thought regretfully of the dazzling sun they had left behind, and of herself and Sam browning their backs on the edge of The Formentor swimming pool.

Sam glanced at her with a sideways smile. Taking one of her hands, he put it on his knee and pressed it.

"Cheer up, my darling. It was a wrench leaving our paradise, but we'll have another holiday as soon as I can afford it."

She put her other hand on top of his, comforted. Then she asked:

"Sam, how rich or how poor *are* we, actually?"

"Well, we're not really poor, darling. I suppose you'd say we belong to the New Poor Rich. That means we aren't really rich either, because we're so heavily taxed. And even though we're going to live simply and you'll do the cooking, etc, we'll still have a lot of expenses. Country life can be almost as dear as life in town. We have to pay off the bills for getting into our house—I may say they've already out-run Uncle Richard's cheque! Then there are things like my fares, commuting to the Stock Exchange, my lunches, and the business entertaining, and our own personal expenditure. The little dinner parties we shall hold, and the odd theatres, will all cost a penny or two. It soon mounts up, doesn't it, and as this is a sticky time for us with so much Left-wing pressure on Tories like ourselves—I dare say we'll find it a bit rough."

"H'm," said Cressida knitting her brows. "I ought to get a job, too. Lots of wives do."

"Not mine, darling. I'd hate it."

"So would I. I want to be a really good housewife," said Cressida. "I don't mind economising, either—I'm so used to it. It's you who will feel the pinch, honey. You've been a gay bachelor for so long."

He laughed.

"A bachelor, but not always gay. Going out to a hell of a lot of meals and parties, playing squash at the club or tearing around Town with some of Franny's Ritzy friends, hasn't been all treacle for me, my love. It's cost me more than I could really afford at times, and I've never ever asked Franny for a cent."

"No, I think you've been wonderful."

"Also, as you know," he went on, "I've only to ask old Guy and he'd cough up, but I wouldn't dream of it. I've got to stand on my own feet and not fall back on my rich step-papa. Besides, he has as much as he can manage settling dear Franny's accounts."

"Isn't it strange," said Cressida, staring ahead as Sam drove deftly through the rather heavy traffic towards the new Chiswick Fly-Over, "how different people can be. How different our mothers' *lives* are! What Franny would spend in an evening playing chemmy at Crockfords, Mummy would have to pinch and scrape for months to accumulate. Then she'd spend it on us—Simon and me."

"Darling, as I've told you before, the Fredas in this life deserve all the honours," he said. "Poor little Franny belongs to a different world and I'm afraid there are plenty of her sort. They are in the minority, of course—but they attach more importance to having fun than more serious things. To Freda it is her family life which is important. So, it will be to me—to *us* . . ." He bent and dropped a kiss on Cressida's hair, but only for the fraction of a second. Sam was a driver who kept his eye on the road . . . "Well no doubt in the fullness of time, *we'll* have to save so as to accumulate some money for our progeny."

"I hope so," said Cressida, her eyes very bright.

She meant it. But she and Sam had discussed the question of having a family and agreed not to start one for a year or two. They were still both young. There was plenty of time. Neither wished to have the burden and responsibility of children until they were fully established—Sam in his job, and she, as a housewife. After all, Sam was the youngest partner in his uncle's firm, and had only recently been what he told her they called a 'Blue Button'—which was a young man right at the bottom of the ladder on the Stock Exchange. She had asked to see the little blue button that these novices wore on the lapels of their coats. Sam had protested when she had said that they might look nice if he could get hold of two and make them into earrings for her.

"They'd hammer me off the Exchange if my wife appeared with their Blue Buttons in her ears," he had answered, roaring with laughter.

As they reached the Fennells' house in Hampstead, Sam drew up at the kerb, took Cressida's hand between his and looked down at her gravely.

"I *have* made you happy these two weeks, haven't I, Cress?"

"Terribly," she nodded vigorously.

"Not been a disappointment?"

Her cheeks burned.

"Heavens no! Everything's been marvellous. You're a wonderful lover as well as a sweet husband."

113

He breathed a sigh of relief. He could still hardly believe that this lovely girl was really his wife and that all was perfect between them. It made it all the more marvellous because she had been so difficult to get.

Sometimes, despite their new intimate relationship, he still found her remote. He did not always quite understand her or her sudden plunges from gaiety down to depression. But Sam was no psychologist and having no complexes in his own nature, did not really try to understand complexity in another person—even Cressida. He left her alone and just told himself that he must be thankful she had married him. She made him utterly happy so long as *she* was happy. As for any financial sacrifices he might have to make in the future, what did he care? His only anxiety was that he should be able to make enough to give her all that she wanted. The very fact that she didn't seem to want much made him doubly anxious to be generous.

"It really has been a blissful honeymoon," he suddenly commented, switching off the engine and putting the key in his pocket. "I fear now we'll have to come down to earth, and listen to Franny's grievances, whatever they might be. Oh well, darling, I'll get on to those 'something-something' electricians and make sure our cooker's connected up so that we can get into our home tomorrow. You'd rather picnic down there in a muddle, than stay up here in comfort, wouldn't you, sweet?"

"I certainly would," she said fervently.

They linked hands as they stood outside the front door of the Fennell home. It was still raining, Cressida had put her white transparent mackintosh over her shoulders and tied a scarf around her hair. She felt as glowing as she looked, she thought. It was good to be in love with the man you had married and it would be such fun when they could get into their own house.

The front door was opened to them by a dark-eyed, dark-haired girl in an overall whom they hadn't seen before. Franny changed her domestic staff as often as she changed her clothes, said Sam. Either she was too particular and they wouldn't stay or they were too particular and wouldn't take the job; he never knew which.

The dark girl greeted them with a Spanish accent which cheered both Sam and Cressida. Their faces lit up. They were at once reminded of all that they had left in Majorca.

"*Buenas Dias!*" said Sam enthusiastically.

"*Ah, hablo Espanola,*" exclaimed the girl her eyes sparkling and broke into a flood of Spanish which neither Sam nor Cressida could understand. She ended up by speaking in broken English, explaining that she was Nina—the new maid.

The Senora was out, she said. The Senor was in bed— very seeck, added Nina, rolling her enormous eyes.

"Oh, dear," said Sam. "Looks like trouble, Cress. Wonder what's wrong with the old boy. We must presume that Franny is having her hair, or her nails, done, or is at a fitting."

"I'll see to the luggage with Nina—you go up and see poor Step-pop," said Cressida, using Sam's private nickname for Guy.

When eventually Sam came out of his stepfather's room and joined Cressida in the spare bedroom, his usually happy faced was troubled.

"I say, I don't like the look of things, darling. The old boy has had a heart attack and he's a very poor colour. His lips are quite blue. Franny didn't let us know, but no . . ." he corrected himself. "She couldn't have done. We couldn't have heard from her. He only had the attack yesterday."

Now they heard Franny's high voice down in the hall. They both went downstairs to meet her. A picture of studied elegance as usual she unwound a chiffon scarf from hair that had obviously just been 'set' as her son had prophesied. There was no smile on the face she lifted for Sam to kiss.

"Thank heavens you're here! I've had an *awful* time!" she began plaintively. "I don't think I've slept all night for worrying. Guy was brought home from the club yesterday semi-conscious and they said he had had this ghastly attack. He called it indigestion, but when Dr. Crispin came, he said it was definitely a coronary, and that he must be kept frightfully quiet or he might have another attack. I wanted him to go straight to the Clinic, but he won't. It's so inconsiderate of him."

"I must say I feel for him," said Sam. "I'd rather be ill in my own home than any hospital."

"I think it's *very* selfish of Guy," said Franny petulantly. "Putting everybody to such trouble here when he can be *well* nursed in the Clinic. Besides, our new Spanish girl has only just arrived and I *know* she'll give notice if she has got to take trays up to Guy's room."

Cressida lit a cigarette and stood by, smoking, marvelling that anybody could be as self-centred as Sam's mother.

In the drawing room, over an aperitif, Franny continued to pour out her personal grievances. Guy's heart attack could *not* have been at a worse time for her! She had planned a *marvellous* party at the River Club and had to cancel it. Then there was the holiday in Portugal they had arranged for next month. Dr. Crispin said Guy wouldn't be able to go. It might mean weeks of complete quiet for him. Crispin was trying to find a good hospital nurse for Guy, but they were very difficult to get hold of—and so on—while Sam and Cressida listened, glancing now and again at each other. Cressida felt so sorry for Sam. He obviously was embarrassed by this exhibition of crass egotism on his mother's part. Cressida could not help thinking of the way her own mother had behaved when her father first went down with that terrible polio. Young though she was then, Cressida had been deeply impressed by her mother's absolute lack of thought for herself. Her one wish in life had been to keep Daddy alive and happy, and even if she had been able to afford to do so, nothing would have induced her to let him exchange his own home for a hospital.

"Is there anything you would like me to do?" Sam asked his mother when she drew breath.

Franny looked through her lashes at her daughter-in-law.

"*You* look very tanned, Cress darling. It suits you," she said irrelevantly.

Death itself would not have destroyed Franny's interest in a woman's appearance, Cressida reflected with irony.

Franny continued:

"How long have you two decided to stay with me?"

"Only one night—and if we're in the way now that poor old Guy is ill, we can move into a hotel," said Sam. "We're going down to Cowfold tomorrow, anyhow."

"And when do you go back to the office?"

"Monday."

"Well, I think it might be useful if you both stayed here for a few days," said Franny with another sly glance at the girl. "I dare say, under the circumstances, darling Cress wouldn't mind lending a hand to Nina; she seems rather a nice girl and I don't want to lose *her* straight away. Of course, she'll probably go anyhow. They all do," she added bitterly. "And as you know, Mrs. Eastman can never get on with *anybody*."

Mrs. Eastman was the cook in this establishment. Sam had lost count of how many cooks had passed through Franny's hands lately, and he never remembered names. But he said quickly:

"Franny dear, I don't think Cress should be asked to help you. We've got to get our own home in order, you know. You have a staff and if you find a nurse for Guy—"

Franny interrupted:

"But Mrs. Eastman has already said she doesn't want to cook for a hospital-nurse. The kitchen *loathes* nurses. You know that, Sam. It's *too* trying."

Cressida, although her heart sank at the prospect, thought now that she ought to make a gesture to Franny, even though she had absolutely no real admiration for her.

"I'll stay if I can be of help, Franny," she said. "I expect we could put off going down to Cowfold for a few days, anyhow, couldn't we, Sam?"

"Oh, *dahling*, how divine of you!" purred Franny.

Sam felt less pleased. He was reluctant to deliver his bride of two weeks into his mother's clutches. He could see that it would be Cress who would do all the really hard jobs; the carrying, the running up and down stairs. He wasn't going to let Franny exploit his wife.

He put an arm around Cressida.

"It's sweet of you, darling—most kind, but I can't allow—" he began.

But Franny interrupted again. She saw that Cressida might be very useful. It would mean that she, herself, could get out more easily if Cress took control. Franny wasn't going to refuse the offer now that it had been made.

She took her tall son by the arm and rubbed her cheek against his shoulder.

"Now don't *you* be selfish, dahling—you've had your little wife all to yourself for two whole weeks—and you've got her for the rest of time—so you can lend her to me for a day or so while Guy is ill."

Sam sighed and capitulated, after which they all went in to lunch. There, they learned that Guy's physician was bringing a specialist along this afternoon. A lot would depend on what he said about Guy.

After lunch, alone in their bedroom, unpacking, Sam grumbled to Cressida.

"Really, Franny is the *end*. I don't see why you should be asked to work in this house. You'll see *she* won't do a darned thing. I know my Franny. She'll make a drama about being terribly anxious and worried and unable to sleep, but it'll only be her own plans she'll worry about. I do wish she'd think of the poor old man—just for once."

Cressida nodded, but knowing that Sam was miserable because his mother behaved this way, she tried to defend her.

"I don't think Franny means to be selfish—it's just her way."

"And it's your way to offer help, and to be so sweet and kind," said Sam, snatching her in his arms and kissing her.

"It isn't really my way at all as I've so often told you—I'm terribly self-centred," Cressida whispered.

"So you're always saying; but I've seen no signs of it. Oh, well, we'll stay here a day or two if Franny needs us so much. But not longer."

"I'll do what I can. You can run down to Cowfold tomorrow, anyhow. If we can just get the cooker organised and the lights going, we'll soon get straight."

"I can't wait," said Sam fervently.

Franny, once she had Cressida in the household as a willing slave, cunningly managed to hand over to her most of the responsibility of coping with the domestic arrangements. If there was one thing Franny hated, it was having to be bothered with such things herself.

Cressida set to work nobly, but found it hard going.

Mrs. Eastman was not a very pleasant woman. She was an excellent cook, but hard-hearted *and* headed—well aware, like all of them these days, that she needn't stay a day longer than she wanted because there were hundreds of well-paid jobs waiting for her. Cressida soon found that Mrs. Eastman had little use for 'Her ladyship' who, she declared, was never punctual, always had more people to meals than she said she would, and was 'that sharp' with Sir Guy, it made her blood boil. Mrs. Eastman liked the old gentleman.

"I'm only staying because of 'im," she confided in young Mrs. Paull. "And I don't go much on that Nina, neither. I don't care for these foreigners. It's all singing and dancing with them and no spit and polish, but I don't blame her if she doesn't want to carry trays up two flights, for neither do I. It's Sir Guy's wife who ought to do it, but *she* wouldn't soil her hands, would her ladyship."

Cressida tried to placate the cook.

"Never mind, Mrs. Eastman. I'll soil mine. I don't mind carrying up trays."

Mrs. Eastman looked at the slim, sunbrowned girl with the air of glowing health, and admired her.

"I must say young Mr. Paull has done himself a bit of good marrying the likes of you and leaving *this* place too," she sniffed. "It won't be long before I leave myself. I can't stand hearing my lady shouting at that poor old gentleman. I wouldn't wonder if it's that what's brought on his heart-trouble and all."

Cressida winced. It might be true, but she wasn't prepared to discuss Sam's mother with Mrs. Eastman. As she left the kitchen, she told herself that trouble was certainly brewing in this beautiful house. A lovely shell of a house without a heart, she thought. Like Sam, she couldn't wait to get down to their own little home—no matter how uncomfortable it might be and with only herself at the kitchen sink!

She telephoned to her mother and was relieved to hear that Daddy had recovered from his cold, that Freda felt rested and was no worse for the wedding, and that all was well with young Simon.

Cressida told Freda that she was going to stay up in town for a day or two in order to help her mother-in-law.

Freda answered:

"You're doing the right thing dear but don't let dear Lady Fennell impose on you—as well she might."

"I won't—you know me!" laughed Cressida.

But she had no idea quite how much she would have to face in Sam's old home during the week that followed. For that very afternoon, while Franny was at Claridges, attending a big Charity Party (Franny was on the committee with a lot of other wealthy, titled women who were amused to give their services and see their names in print) catastrophe befell the Hampstead house.

Guy Fennell did not live to see the heart-specialist.

Cressida looked in to see if he was all right, soon after Franny left home. She found the old man in his pyjamas, lying on the floor. He had obviously got out of bed and been seized by a second and, this time, fatal thrombosis.

Cressida screamed for Sam. They telephoned Dr. Crispin. He was out. By the time they found a local physican to come and give first aid to Sir Guy, it was too late.

Guy had already gone beyond help.

It was a shock for Cressida and Sam was deeply distressed that she should have been so involved. But this was where he saw his young wife in a new light. The often nervy, moody Cressida became a strong, resourceful woman. She handled everything and everybody—including her mother-in-law—with a composure that astonished even her adoring husband.

It was no mean task, having to cope with Franny. When the news of Guy's sudden death was broken to her by her son and she realised that she was a widow for the second time, she became wildly hysterical.

"Oh, my God, *my God*, oh poor Guy . . . oh Sam—and what will become of *me*? It's too terrible! I can't go through this all again. It was bad enough when your father died! Why should I have such ghastly luck?" She began to cry and moan, clinging on to Sam while the tears played havoc with her make-up.

Cressida thought: Even at a time like this, it's herself she's really bothering about. She's fantastic!

Franny then flung herself on to the sofa and began to scream in earnest. Sam looked on aghast, helpless. Like most men, he did not know really what to do in this sort of situation. The Hampstead doctor who had been with Guy had left. Sam tried to contact Guy's own medical adviser again.

"Ring the specialist, too, darling," suggested Cressida. "You'd better stop him coming."

"Oh, lord, yes! . . ." muttered Sam.

Franny threw herself at Cressida.

"You don't know what I've suffered in my life! When Sam's father died, I had everything to see to. I was all alone. Now history is repeating itself. Oh, if I'd *dreamed* Guy had a serious heart-weakness, I wouldn't have married him—" she broke off and coughed and wept into her handkerchief.

Cressida was shocked, but dealt firmly with her.

"You'd better come upstairs to your own room, Franny," she said. "I expect Dr. Crispin will come in a moment and give you a sedative. Meanwhile, we'll find you some Disprin or something. You must lie down and keep quiet."

"I can't," cried Franny. "My room communicates with Guy's. He's lying in there. It's horrible. I can't bear it."

She burst into a fresh flood of tears.

God, what a woman, thought Cressida grimly.

"Then you can come up to our room which is the other side of the house and nowhere near Sir Guy," she said, and helped Franny there. She unzipped the woman's dress, found her a dressing-gown, got her into it somehow, and made her lie down. Franny, hiccupping and sobbing, told her where to find a bottle of Disprin. Cressida gave her two.

She left her for a moment and went downstairs to order tea. She found Mrs. Eastman alone. To do the cook justice, she was in tears and genuinely upset.

"Isn't it shocking, Miss, I mean Madam . . . that *poor* old gentleman . . . and I could hear her ladyship carrying on, although I bet she's not crying for *him*. She'll be wondering what's in the Will."

This was too much for Cressida.

"Mrs. Eastman, you shouldn't say things like that," she began sternly.

"Excuse me and what did I say about them foreign maids," added Mrs. Eastman, triumphantly. "When that Nina heard that Sir Guy had dropped dead, did *she* offer to help? No, she fainted on me and then put on her things and walked out, she did. She said she was going to some Spanish convent where her friends are and that she wouldn't be back until Sir Guy had gone. She wasn't going to sleep in a house with a corpse, she said, although I couldn't really understand half she *did* say."

Oh goodness, thought Cressida, what a crowd they are. *Poor* Sam. Thank goodness he hasn't got to tackle all this without me.

She calmed Mrs. Eastman down, told her not to worry, that she would help her tonight, and fetch Nina back tomorrow when Sir Guy's body would have been taken away. She then made the tea, herself, and carried a tray up to her mother-in-law.

Things were better once Dr. Crispin arrived on the scene. He knew Lady Fennell. He dealt with her accordingly and before long she was sleeping under a strong sedative.

Crispin seemed distressed, but not surprised by the news of Sir Guy's sudden fatal collapse. He told Sam that the old man's heart had been very rocky.

It was a subdued and rather sad homecoming for Sam and Cressida. The honeymoon was indeed over, but they forgot themselves and their own plans and gave Franny their loyal support.

Until the funeral, they stayed up in the Hampstead house which was a considerable sacrifice for Cressida. The one thing she longed for was to get down to Cowfold. Sam went down there and told her when he got back that the electrical work had now been completed. It made her feel all the more restive.

"But I don't see how we can leave Franny. She seems rather in a state of shock," Sam said.

Cressida kept quiet. Sam was a dear, blind old owl at times, she thought with affection. He liked to imagine that he knew his mother, but he didn't; he didn't really dream quite what a despicable character she was. Just as well. Perhaps he didn't want to see the truth, but Cressida noted that the 'state of shock' didn't prevent dear Franny from going out—ordering the most attractive black silk suit which she showed Cressida with suitable sniffs of sorrow and a little black hat with a black veil to tie under her chin which would make her look ravishing at the funeral.

But Franny clung to Cressida, and in a fit of generosity even gave her a charming little enamel watch set in brilliants which had been a wedding present from Sam's father. It had a diamond brooch pin.

"I never wear pin-on watches—you might as well have it," Franny said carelessly.

Cressida didn't really want to take it, but she knew that Sam would like her to have the watch. She had to admit it was a beautiful thing and she liked to think it had been chosen by Sam's own father. Franny, once back in the house, showed up at her worst. Cressida had listened to so many outpourings and contradictions from her mother-in-law that she could hardly believe that all those tears she shed by the graveside were genuine. She had put on a good show. She had to be supported by her son and Guy's solicitor, Mr. Nugent, who was a family friend. Then they all retired to the dining room where the Will was to be read to them by Mr. Nugent.

This was where Franny went right out of control. Cressida had never been more sorry for Sam.

The contents of the Will startled them all. Mr. Nugent unfolded the facts rather apologetically.

"Er—you all have—er—of course, looked upon the late Sir Guy as a man of substance—of wealth—but such was not the case and although, of course, I was in his confidence and knew about it, he did not wish Lady Fennell to be bothered with it in his lifetime. Ahem . . ." Mr. Nugent cleared his throat and shuffled the papers on the dining-room table, around which the family were sitting. "I'm really very sorry indeed, but I am afraid you, Lady Fennell, will have to face a considerable change of fortune."

Franny sat like a frozen figure, twisting her black chiffon handkerchief between her fingers, and with her large, long-lashed eyes staring a little wildly at the solicitor.

"I don't know what you mean," at last she breathed the words.

He soon told her.

Guy Fennell was one of two brothers—the younger, Colonel Peter Fennell had been killed in the Second World War. At that time Guy had lost his own father and inherited the baronetcy, but the title had carried with it little save a decaying castle somewhere in Wales which had since passed to the National Trust, and only a small estate. Like Sam, Guy found himself with a stepfather. His mother had married again at the ripe age of seventy, a man named George Pickering who was a wealthy, retired grocer from the Midlands. This fact had been kept very quiet by Guy's old mother because of her sudden drop in the social scale. When Mr. Pickering died, he left between four and five hundred thousand pounds to his wife and stepson, but the conditions of the Will were not simple. It stipulated that after Guy, himself, died, the money should pass back to the Pickering family. This consisted of three nephews—all living in or near Birmingham. When the late Lady Fennell (then Mrs. Pickering) died, Guy was in control of his stepfather's fortune. Mr. Nugent pointed out to Sam and Franny, Sir Guy had been well aware that he could not leave this money to Franny, but he dared not tell her so.

Somewhat embarrassed, Mr. Nugent added that Sir Guy had kept these matters secret rather than upset his beautiful wife whom he had adored when first he married her. But he also knew that he would never leave her penniless because he still had the Fennell money. This, of course, was no fortune. It was nearer to forty thousand pounds which would only bring in an income of little over a thousand a year after taxes and death duties were paid.

Sam looked anxiously at his mother. Franny was deathly white under her make-up. Her lips were trembling. Her whole body shook. There followed a regrettable scene which made Cressida feel that she would like to run out of the house. But this was a time when she knew she must stay. She must help poor Sam.

The other mourners, friends and relatives, who had come in for a glass of wine left the house. Two cousins of Guy's had come from the North and Franny's great friends, Colin and Meryl Ryvingdon, paid their respects but left the family hastily.

Colin, after hearing about the Will, said to his wife that it 'served that little spendthrift right.' Meryl indignantly defended Franny. She thought Sir Guy had behaved atrociously by not warning Franny of this state of affairs. Poor Fran had always imagined she would be left very well off.

"Serve her right," Colin repeated. "She's damned extravagant and she made that poor chap's life a hell once she got him *and* the title."

Alone with her son and daughter-in-law and the solicitor, Franny continued to rant and revile her dead husband. She had no conscience about her own behaviour or the fact that she had married Guy for money rather than love. She could think of nothing except that she had been 'grossly deceived'. Why should Guy's fortune go to these Pickerings, whoever they were?

The lawyer pointed out that it was Pickering money in the first place and that Sir Guy's stepfather had a right to leave it to whom he chose; also that Guy had really been lucky to have the use of it in his lifetime. Franny exploded again.

"I've been wickedly misled. What's the good of a thousand a year to *me*? It won't even pay my staff wages. I'll have to sell this house *and* the Rolls and everything else of value. I'll have nothing. It's iniquitous. Oh, I never dreamed that Guy would do such a wicked thing!"

Mr. Nugent did not dare look at Lady Fennell's livid little face. He had had many a talk with his late client over the past year or two and realised how Lady Fennell tried to fleece him. Mr. Nugent felt scant pity for her.

Sam didn't feel much pity, either. He felt deeply ashamed, but his innate kindness led him to go to her now and put a comforting arm around her.

"Franny dear—don't upset yourself like this, please. It won't do any good. I don't think poor old Guy meant to treat you badly. He was just afraid to tell you about the Pickerings and his stepfather's Will."

"Don't try and smooth it over—" Franny pushed her son away. Real tears now of rage and resentment were pouring down her cheeks.

She continued to say what she thought of the husband she

had only just buried; Cressida felt sick, but sat beside Sam smoking, speechless. She wondered, not without cause, whether Mrs. Eastman and Nina were outside the door listening avidly to their mistress's shrill voice.

There followed a further hour of futile protests and recriminations from Franny, of good advice from Mr. Nugent, and vain attempts by Sam to pacify his mother. By the time they sent for the over-worked Dr. Crispin and got him to quieten Franny down, they were all exhausted.

Later that night, after Franny was asleep, Sam and Cressida went out for a walk. Sam announced grimly that he needed fresh air. It was a fine warm night. Arm in arm, bare-headed, the young Paulls strolled through the now quiet streets of Hampstead. Cressida kept glancing at Sam's profile anxiously. She had never seen him look so stern.

"Oh, darling," she said, "I am *terribly* sorry this has happened. It must be awful for you."

"Don't mind about me, love. It's Franny. She's behaved very badly indeed and I don't mind saying so. I know she hasn't much control, but I do think she could have been a little less virulent about the old man, seeing as how he is not yet cold in his grave, and gave her so much while he lived."

"I expect it's been a terrible shock to her."

"What a ghastly power money has over human beings," muttered Sam. "It makes one want to get rid of every penny and go and live on a desert island—back to the primeval days when you didn't have to buy your food or clothing—you just went out and hunted for them."

"I'm afraid, darling, there are very few such islands left," sighed Cressida. "The whole world has become money-minded."

"Well, I certainly knew nothing about the Pickerings," said Sam. "The old man kept it pretty quiet. I suppose he fell for Franny so badly in the first place that he thought he would get her by fair means or foul. When all is said and done, I suppose he *ought* to have been frank with her over the money."

"Even so, darling, a thousand a year free of income tax seems a jolly lot to me. But I suppose that's because my family never had much more and brought us up on it—Simon and myself."

Sam pressed her arm to his side. His face softened as he looked down at her.

"Darling Cress! We can hardly say *we're* very well off, either. But I know you don't mind. That's the blessed part about you."

"I'm not used to luxury. Poor Franny is. It will be rather a come-down for her."

"The problem now is what we are going to do with her, let alone what will she do, herself. She was dead right when she said that she'll have to sell everything of value. There can be no more of the mink-and-diamond life for our Fran. It'll mean a small flat and economy for her, I fear."

Now Cressida, ever conscious of what she owed her husband and still guilt-ridden, made the biggest gesture of her life.

"If you want Franny to live with us in our house—I mean we've got a spare room and—"

But Sam did not let her finish.

"*God*, no! That's the last thing, darling! It would never work, having Franny with us. She'd drive us both mad. Besides, our way of life is fairly simple, and it could never be hers. She loathes the country. Thanks all the same, sweetie. It was terrific of you to offer."

If Cressida felt relieved, she didn't say so. But as she walked along with Sam, her mind worked busily and she could foresee that the future regarding Franny might hold quite a few personal problems for them all. Franny would want a lot of helping, and looking after, and perhaps at times, even need financial assistance from the son she had so long neglected. Sam's attitude towards her had always been charitable, but charity was a word which Franny did not understand in its true meaning.

Then Sam put an arm around Cressida's waist and pulled her closer to him.

"Come along, let's go home. You must be worn out. I can only apologise for dragging you into this family mêlée. I must say it's been a rotten end to our honeymoon and a great shock losing poor Guy like this."

"We can take it," she smiled up at him.

"I do love you," he said irrelevantly.

"I love you," she echoed.

Then suddenly the one thing that Cressida couldn't 'take' loomed up in her life again. Sam said:

"Whatever happens, we must get down to our own home. After all, you can stay there and get it in order. I know Freda will help you and I'll come home most nights. But I'll have to give Franny what time I can. How about us contacting old Dom and asking him to come down for the week-end and give us a hand? I expect he'd like it—if he's in town still."

Cressida froze and moved away from Sam.

"No," she said abruptly . . . "I mean I don't want anybody until the house is straight. Freda and I'll manage and Simon's still home—he'll help us."

Sam appeared not to notice that the atmosphere was suddenly tense. He went on:

"You'll understand if I have to look after Franny a bit until I can find someone to take over, won't you, darling? She has a cousin in London, a Mrs. Wilkins—known in the family as Cousin Coot, for some reason or other. She wasn't at the funeral. She's a sensible and quite clever woman—a widow. I rather like her, but Fran's never been very nice to her because she isn't in her set. She's hard up, but I think Franny would find Coot useful now, especially as she actually read Law when she was a girl, so she'll be invaluable just at the moment. She could advise Franny and tackle Mr. Nugent about the Will, and Insurances, and so forth. At least poor old Guy did insure his life, so Franny will get *that*. And I reckon she'll want it. I'm damn sure there'll be a hell of a lot of outstanding bills to settle."

Cressida listened, but her mind was not on the subject of Franny or Cousin Coot. She was thinking of Dominic. That name still had such power to hurt, to move, to destroy her peace of mind, she thought distractedly. She wondered if she was ever going to get away from him. She felt deeply depressed as she and Sam walked back to the house.

10

THE September morning was dull and muggy. It had been raining all night which fact upset Cressida because there was nothing much in the neglected garden of 'Dorians'—her new home—save old rose bushes. The heavy downpour, hour after hour, had destroyed most of the blooms; they had opened wide in the sun yesterday, but now the beds were strewn with petals.

Cressida stood at her kitchen sink. She found, like all her friends, that she spent a great deal of her time there these days. She was preparing a fish dish. She disliked the smell of fish cooking, but Sam was fond of cold fish mayonnaise in the summer. Cressida struggled with a cookery book. Freda had helped a lot since they had taken possession of 'Dorians'. But this morning Freda was busy—preparing a party for Simon who was still on holiday and had invited some of his young friends to supper.

Cressida could hear the hum of a Hoover in the bedroom overhead. Mrs. Parsloe was turning the room out. She was quite a character, was Mrs. Parsloe, nearing seventy, wiry and still active. She had one great-grandchild who had been born only a week ago and called 'Samuel' after her new employer. Despite the fact that Mrs. Parsloe had only been with the Paulls for a month, she was, as Cressida told everybody, dead nuts on Mr. Paull who pulled her leg. He was always telling her how attractive she still was. This badinage was generally received by a high cackle of laughter from Mrs. Parsloe.

"He's ever such a gentleman," she told everybody in the village, "and I don't care what they say about England going Labour—I'm a Conservative, meself, and have always worked for the gentry, and always will and that's a fact!"

Cressida was quite settled now in her new home. Except for her innate opposition to cooking—she was content. She was always busy. She was still making curtains. She was fond of the garden, too, and liked to weed and plant and she was delighted with all that she and Sam had so far achieved with the décor in rooms that needed a lot more spent on them than they could afford.

They were both proud of 'Dorians' and of its history. Already they had found out that the house had been built while the Prince Regent was still on the throne, and that buried in the village church there was a Lord Cecil Dorian who had been a famous Regency rake. It was presumed that His Lordship had installed some of his many mistresses, if not his wife, in this charming period place *en route* for 'Brighthelmstone'. But since those days, 'Dorians' had been almost ruined by ugly Victorian additions which Sam swore he would pull down one day. When the old lady who had lived here for forty years died, her executors put the place on the market. Because of complete neglect and a certain amount of dry rot, cracked plaster and peeling papers, the whole property had such a forlorn look that it had dropped in value.

Quite a lot had been done to smarten it up now. Electricity, a new hot water system and a new bathroom had been installed. Sam and Cressida had had the drawing room, dining room and their own bedroom redecorated, and a new unit put in the old-fashioned kitchen where they also intended to eat most of their meals when alone. There was still a lot to be done, as Cressida kept noting. However, it would be fun to do it. Already she and Sam adored the place. But, of course, Guy's death had been a setback.

It was the end of the month. Tomorrow would be the first of October.

Ever since their marriage, Sam, much against his will, had inevitably been forced to give most of his spare time to his mother rather than his wife. Cressida was very good about it. She knew that Sam couldn't help it—Franny had dug her claws into him, and the week-ends when he had longed to be at 'Dorians', working in house or garden, had had to be given to Hampstead where he struggled to put the Fennells' affairs in order. A Herculean task, as he told Cressida. He looked tired and harassed. It was hot in London and Franny had been hysterical and more self-centred than ever since her fortunes so suddenly declined. Sam, for once, was short-tempered himself.

As he had feared, his mother would have only a small income once probate was granted. Already he had had to put the house on the market and help Franny dispose of some of her most valuable jewellery. He was also trying—still without success—to find her a small flat in town. She was so difficult. Utterly spoiled, she did not want to move away from what she called 'a good address', and rents in the best places were quite beyond her new means.

She continued to revile Guy. She had begun to undermine even Sam's filial devotion and understanding by constantly hinting that it was a pity *he*, Sam, got married when he did, because if he had been free now, she could have made a home with *him*.

When Sam had mentioned this to Cressida, he added:

"God forbid that I should ever have had to share a home with our Franny. You came into my life just in time to save me, my darling!"

"I hope you'll always feel like that," Cressida had answered.

The past still haunted Cressida although she had been so busy lately with mundane domestic affairs that she hadn't had much time to feel the old sense of guilt about Dominic. Besides which, Dominic himself was out of England. Urgent business had recalled him to Brazil. Because of it, he had had to break away from his new partnership in the theatre. Cressida was thankful when she heard this but, of course, she did not know when Sam might suddenly bring 'old Dom' back into her life.

This morning she felt a queer sense of foreboding as well as depression. Things never really went smoothly in this life, she reflected. All this business about Guy and Franny had cast a definite gloom over her marriage. Sam rushed back to her, passionately eager to be with her—just as much her lover as ever. But the fatigue of carrying out his normal duties on the Stock Exchange, and rushing between mother and wife, was beginning to tell on him. Cressida felt the repercussions. Sam was so tired sometimes that he fell asleep as soon as his head touched the pillow. He kept apologising to her for his lassitude. He was also obviously very worried about money. As he had suspected, Franny's debts were frightening. Almost every penny they could collect after the sale of house and jewellery had to be distributed among her creditors. The famous Cousin Coot had come up to scratch and rallied to Franny's side. She was living with her now. Because she was neither smart nor amusing, Franny complained bitterly to Sam that she found her 'a crashing bore'. She grumbled at and bullied Coot and Sam told Cressida that he was afraid that even Coot's angelic nature and adoration of Franny wouldn't stand up to things for long. What he didn't tell her was how often his mother pointed out to him bitterly that he should have married Diana. She could have done with a wealthy daughter-in-law now, she said.

Sam was furious with her at these times and forbade her to say such things, but Franny was not to be silenced. Sam found himself going through a very trying time.

Cressida didn't complain when finally he told her that they must cancel their plans to install central heating this autumn. He wasn't making much money at the moment and he might even have to help Franny with her new rent once she found a place to move into. This brought a protest from Cressida despite her wish to be the ideal and sympathetic wife.

"Honestly, darling, I don't see why you should give your mother a penny. She's never done a thing for you—on your own admission. I know what you're going to say—she is, after all, your *mother*. Yes, but she isn't *destitute*. She's still got a thousand a year for life which some people would call riches. It's only her old standard and extravagance that make her feel that she can't manage."

Sam looked gloomy.

"I suppose it wouldn't be fair on you if I help her, but don't be cross with me," he said. "I can't help it."

"Of course you can't. And it isn't only a question of being unfair to me. It's unfair on *you*. That's what I resent."

"I can take it," he said.

"Well, I can't."

"I don't want you to have to take it," Sam muttered crossly. "Very soon you'll wish you hadn't married me."

Silence fell between them. They stared at each other rather miserably. This little scene had taken place last night. Cressida, while she cooked this morning, was remembering it and how it had upset her. She supposed that one shouldn't make an idol of anybody in this life. Sam had seemed so wonderful— so god-like, but even he was proving only human and his marvellous good humour and unselfishness were being strained by the present situation. She wouldn't have minded if he had wanted to economise in the cause of helping a really deserving relative, but it went against the grain with Cressida to be asked to do without her central heating in this cold, draughty old house because of *Franny*.

Little more was said about it, but for the first time, Cressida had felt the sudden dropping of a veil between Sam and herself—a very fine veil but it was there, nevertheless, dimming the radiance and ardour they had felt together in Majorca.

Cressida went to see her mother and father this afternoon, but would not have dreamed of telling them about the delicate situation. They both knew, of course, that Franny had lost all her money, but neither of them imagined that Sir Guy's Will would affect Cressida. She spent a pleasant afternoon at the bungalow and once back at 'Dorians' felt a new thrill of pride and pleasure in her own house. The sun had come out. The roses looked beautiful again and she decided that it would be extremely silly to let Franny's misfortunes come between Sam and herself, in even a minor fashion.

Poor Sam! It was all such bad luck on him! She knew that the last thing he would want was to rob *her*, his wife, of a penny. It was a shame. She would put on one of her new trousseau dresses and welcome him tonight with starry eyes, and make him forget his troubles. He really had been looking so drawn and heavy-eyed lately. She must make him forget Franny and the money, and become once more, her ardent lover of the honeymoon. She had really missed their passionate moments—their complete absorption in each other. As a bride of only eight or nine weeks, she could not allow Sam to turn into a dreary husband, too tired and harassed for love, she told herself dryly.

She was confident that she looked her most alluring once

she finished dressing. She chose a maize-gold silky linen dress, which had no sleeves and clung to her narrow waist. With this, she put on white sandals. She wore no stockings—her legs were still brown from the Spanish sun. Her silky dark hair had grown long since her marriage. She pinned it up high on her head this evening. It gave her a rather exotic look. Sam loved it like this. She was trying out a new rich shade of lipstick and nail varnish.

She slipped into an overall. In the pretty lilac and white kitchen with its shining white enamel unit she set to work to lay the supper. She was going to give Sam a jellied soup before the fish mayonnaise, and the excellent little grocer in Cowfold had found a nice ripe Brie for them.

She decided to use the lilac linen cloth tonight with the black flowers on it, which, with napkins to match, had been Julia Chalmers' wedding present. Just as she was spreading it, Cressida heard the scrunch of car wheels in the drive. A very dilapidated drive, as she and Sam well knew; but they could not afford to have anything done for the moment, so weeds and holes remained.

She took off her overall and ran out to meet her husband.

But it was not Sam—nor the little Triumph Herald. It was the big white Mercedes. Dominic Miln walked towards the front door. Dominic wore grey slacks, a dark blue shirt and a silk scarf which he took off and waved at her.

"Hello there!"

She stood speechless. She had been expecting this, yet not expecting it. Not tonight anyhow. She felt a mixture of resentment and pleasure. Yet she couldn't quite kill the old feeling of excitement that the sight of Dominic had always aroused in her. It really was a case, she thought, of loving and hating at the same time. The only thing that she firmly believed was that her hatred of him prevailed. His was now the fascination of the snake. She was afraid of it even while she felt its strange allure.

"Sorry I didn't let you know I was coming," he said. "I couldn't even contact Sam. I tried to, but he wasn't in the office and they said he'd gone off early. I thought perhaps he was here helping the little wife to weed the garden or something so I drove straight down to see you. As a matter of fact, I only flew back from Brazil this afternoon."

"Come in do," she said awkwardly.

He stood still a moment in the sunshine.

She saw his gaze wander around and knew that he, at least, was not one of those people who mind the dilapidated state of house or garden. The artist in him would rejoice— as she did—in all that was unspoiled about the little Regency house. The beautiful panelled door with the Georgian fanlight over it. The noble proportions; the high garden walls built of pinkish-grey bricks, half covered now with a tangle of climbing roses and jasmine on one side and a row of ancient, overgrown espalier pears and peaches, facing south. At least the grass had been cut. The lawn looked velvety despite the moss and weeds; and there were two glorious tulip trees on either side of the house which added greatly to the attraction. As Cressida expected, Dominic broke into raptures.

"What a divine little house! How lucky you are to have found it."

"Yes—we only got it by a fluke. Sam happened to walk into the agent's the very day it came on the market otherwise it would have been snapped up, although it needed a terrible lot doing to it and still does. It could cost the earth if one let oneself go, but we're having to do it all gradually."

He looked at her. She knew that look. It made her cheeks burn. She turned restlessly away from his searching eyes.

"Come in," she repeated abruptly. "I'll give you a drink. Sam should be here at any moment."

"It's you I've really come to see."

"Don't be silly," she snapped.

He laughed.

She took him into the sitting room and began to behave like a formal hostess, introducing him to her new home. She explained things; the pelmet hadn't come yet; she hoped he liked the yellow and grey chintz curtains; it was lucky that they had found this polished parquet floor, so far they had only got two or three Persian rugs which had come from Sam's old flat. That sofa, they had bought second hand. The covers, to match the curtains, were still being made. And wasn't that a nice old walnut bureau? Guy Fennell had given it to them. And so on until Dominic interrupted:

"Steady on—you're not trying to let the house to me you know, you funny Little Cat."

Cressida turned on him furiously.

"I won't have you use that name!"

Dominic seated himself on the arm of the sofa, took a packet of cigarettes from his coat pocket and handed them to her. When she shook her head, he lit a cigarette and smiled up at her flushed, angry young face.

"Oh Cressida, Cressida, my sweet, how changed you are! I used to admire you because you seemed as bored by formalities and clichés and all the other emblems of civilisation as I was. I'm a primitive, so were you in Rome. *Must* you become Mrs. Samuel Paull with her nice husband, her nice home, her nice manners and her nice principles. Must you pretend that all the splendid truths and realities you once believed in and lived by, no longer exist?"

"They don't exist as far as I'm concerned."

"I find that hard to believe. I remember how bored you used to be because Madame La Duchessa was always following the fashions and refusing to flaunt the conventions. And you complained that life in your own home was so restricted. Are you now definitely restricting yourself to your pleasant marriage living as thousands of other little pleasant housewives who have to find their excitement in heart throb romances or television?"

Cressida bit at her lower lip, but kept her head high and tried to look into his amused eyes with a conviction she was so afraid she lacked.

"That's all I am—a pleasant housewife," she said defiantly, "and all I want to be. And I like my pleasant marriage with my nice husband, thank you very much."

"You do look gorgeous, darling," he said suddenly irrelevantly. "Your Majorcan honeymoon, plus the summer sun down here—what you've had of it—has given you that same wonderful, golden tan that you had in Rome. I always forget until I see you again how green your eyes are. You really must sit for me again and let me paint the pleasant housewife of

136

Cowfold. What a delicious name—Cowfold! It conjures up a wonderful new rural picture of my mad Little Cat That Was."

She set her teeth.

"I'm glad you say *that was*. I'm certainly not your Little Cat any longer. I belong to Sam."

"Darling Cressida," he said, "I wouldn't dream of trying to filch you from my old Cambridge chum. I'm not really as unprincipled as that."

"I'm not so sure!"

"And I'm not so sure you haven't still got a tiny spark of the old feeling left for me," he said.

"You have a big idea of yourself. Anyhow, I don't understand you."

"Oh, yes, you do. You understood me in Rome very well. We were very close."

"You're fantastic!" she exclaimed with a gasp. "You are Sam's friend. You were his Best Man and you know that I wish Rome had never happened—why do you go on saying this sort of thing to me? Why do you want to come down here and upset me?"

He continued to smoke, coolly, smiling.

"My dearest Cressida, I'm relieved to hear that I still have the power to upset you—if you didn't still feel a spark, you wouldn't be upset, would you?"

"I think you're atrocious and if Sam knew—" she began.

"But Sam doesn't know," Dominic broke in softly.

"You really have no morals, have you?"

"None. I never did have any. You know that."

She started to say something else, but stopped. She hadn't the least idea what to say to this man. She could only be furious with herself, because he did, indeed, seem to have power to move her, even to anger. Dominic spoke again;

"Let's not waste time by snarling at each other, my darling. Sam has married you—this is your home. I'm the guest, even if an unwelcome one. I'll try to behave. Let's be friends."

"Sam will welcome you, I'm sure," Cressida said rather bitterly.

Dominic put out a hand to her.

"Friends?"

"Not really," she said, her cheeks crimson again, her lashes nervously flickering, "you must realise how embarrassing it is for me to see you."

"Isn't it rather fun to be embarrassed?"

"No."

"Darling," he laughed, "you ought by virtue of your *name* to be ready for any infidelity."

She stared at him.

"My name? I don't know what you mean."

"I was looking up the meaning of certain names the other day. Shakespeare used Cressida, of course, but did you ever know its old derivation?"

She shook her head. She thought: *He bewilders me. He always did.*

Nobody could deal with Dominic. He was quick-silver. His brain worked with such astonishing swiftness and rapid change of thought. He could never be pinned down. (She ought to know that after Rome.) Nothing she could say would have any effect upon him. If he wanted to go on seeing and embarrassing her—he would do so. He got up from the sofa and began to pace up and down the drawing room, moving in that graceful, rather panther-like way that she remembered; he was telling her about her name. How the original had been spelt *Criseida*. She, according to Greek mythology, was the daughter of Chryses—a priest of Apollo. Agamenon returned her to her father at the command of the god because of her infidelities. Her name had become a by-word of faithlessness.

Cressida listened to this with downcast eyes. Her face still burning, but her lips curled disdainfully. She decided that the best way to deal with Dominic was not to take him seriously or be stupidly prudish in his presence.

"I'm sure if my parents had realised that, they would have called me by some other name. And what does *your* name mean, dear Dominic? Could it possibly stand for fidelity?" she asked.

"*Darling*, don't sneer—it doesn't suit you. Actually my name—which in Brazil they call *Domingo*—is a very Catholic one and used by the monks in honour of St. Dominic."

"How suitable," said Cressida with a freezing smile.

He shook his head at her.

"You have indeed changed. But ravishing to look at, I must say. What about a gin, my pet?"

"I'll get one for you," she said. "Sam can't be long now."

"Are you going to feed the unwelcome guest?"

"Stay to supper by all means," she called back. "There isn't much. I never was a cook, as you know."

"I never asked you to cook," his voice followed her into the hall. "I used to take you out to all those divine little cafés where we would eat our scampi and drink our *vin du pays*."

She collected glasses from the dining-room cupboard and found gin and French Vermouth, remembering all too well that that was what he liked to drink before dinner. Then she went into the kitchen to pull a tray of ice-cubes out of the fridge.

She had been living in a cosy little domesticated world lately, she reflected—a world in which Dominic played no part. She had been so fully occupied, she hadn't really given him or the past a thought. This evening the very sight of him, and sound of that slow attractive voice reminded her all too vividly of those fantastic days in Rome. It hadn't been at all 'cosy' then—sharing life with Dominic. On the contrary, she had led a mad, feverish kind of existence when she alternated between passionate, rapturous happiness and the awful haunting fear she used to have of losing him. Then, he had been the very centre of her dreams. She had placed him on a pedestal—even while she knew that one day he must surely fall from it. She had never felt like that about Sam. She was absolutely sure of him. Perhaps that was a bad thing—to be too sure of anyone. Perhaps it destroyed some of the excitement that was part and parcel of absolute passion even though it was the essence of absolute love.

Dominic's very inaccessibility had lent some sort of extra value to him. She could see that now very clearly. Since then, *she* had become the inaccessible one, by virtue of her marriage. Was it that which attracted him to her now?

How vile man is, she decided rather dramatically as she ran the hot water over the ice tray and shook the loosened cubes into the glass bucket with the silver rim and handle which had been one of Sam's wedding presents. She, too, must count herself as having been unscrupulous in her conduct—carried away by her overwhelming desire for Dominic. That terrible, terrible longing to be with him which like a magnet had drawn her to his studio again and again.

She felt weak and angry in a curiously impotent way when she carried the tray of drinks in to Dominic. He did not seem to notice it. He sipped his drink, lit another cigarette and walked round the room, stopping to admire the Bristol glass, that flashing blue fire on the mantelpiece. He was less admiring of the oil painting which Sam had hung over the walnut bureau.

"Ah, Dieppe! The old port. I recognise it," he said. "Quite good colour, but not up to your standard, Cressida."

She remained silent. He seemed determined to try and re-establish the old link of ideas and tastes once shared between them. He went on:

"An unknown artist, I presume. Your choice or Sam's? I don't like the way he or she puts on the paint. It's too thick. So many young painters try to copy Van Gogh and fail miserably."

"It isn't a young painter," she spoke suddenly glad to be able to contradict him. "It's an elderly aunt of Sam's who used to go over to Dieppe and do a lot of painting, as a matter of fact."

Dominic turned to her with one of his sudden flashing smiles.

"I didn't really think it was *you*. By the time I'd finished with you, you knew a bit more about the noble art of painting than the average girl. You were an apt pupil, darling."

She poured herself out a drink and wished her fingers wouldn't shake.

"Oh, was I?"

"Darling, don't pretend. I do so hate what is known as, putting on a face. We don't have to deceive each other, you and I. I know you are Sam's wife, but once you and I were lovers and—"

"Oh, be quiet. You have no scruples," she interrupted, and glared at him.

He laughed and raised his glass to her.

"Here's to your green cat's eyes. How they flash when you're angry. Do you often flash them at your husband? The poor fellow must find it very disturbing."

"You're impossible," she muttered.

"Tell me something—are you trying to deny to yourself that you ever loved me?"

"It wasn't love—it was infatuation," she said.

Now he laughed again—quite loudly and flung back his head.

"Oh, angel, *really*! You have become too, *too* respectable. Clichés just drop like imitation pearls out of your beautiful mouth. A very beautiful mouth, I always thought. But you haven't grown up yet, Mrs. Paull, that's obvious. You were always rather naïve, but you are married now, and surely you admit a girl can have had a past and need not be ashamed of it. You seem overcome with remorse. You're behaving like a prudish old maid. Are you terrified of facing up to the word 'sin'?"

Cressida set her glass down on the table. She looked up at him with genuine astonishment.

"I simply don't understand you, Dominic. I'm not a prude and I'm not an old maid and I'm *not* afraid to face up to 'sin'. But I do believe there are certain decencies, and I think it's positively indecent, the way you're always harping back on what happened between us in Rome."

"Have you forgotten it?"

"No," she said, her cheeks hot and her breath uneven. "Certainly not. But I don't want to think about it. I love Sam. I'm married to him and this is our home. I don't know how you can call yourself his friend and say these things to me."

Dominic sighed.

"All very right and proper, of course, but you disappoint me."

"You're stupid and very disloyal to Sam," she broke out furiously. "What are you trying to do, anyhow? Upset us both?"

Dominic sat down again, folded his arms and went on smiling at her in that amused way which made her feel so stupidly angry and helpless.

"Of course not, my dear girl; I don't even pretend to myself that I *could* upset you. You're a nice happily married couple. You can remain so. You can be a dear good suburban little wife. But nothing can destroy the memory of the Cressida you used to be when you were mine."

She coloured.

"You're very perverse, Dominic. You didn't even really want me in Rome—certainly not at the end—did you? Oh, I know you always said you'd walk out one day, and you did. It hurt me at the time. But it's over. Why want to start things up again?"

He looked at her through half shut eyes.

"Perhaps one doesn't always realise the true value of a thing until you've lost it."

"Now *you're* talking in clichés," she taunted him.

He ignored this.

"You were so sweet in Rome. The whole thing was rather wonderful while it lasted."

Oh, God, she thought, how much longer is he going on like this. Sam will be back at any moment. I don't want *him* to be upset. I can't cope with Dominic.

He held out his empty glass to her.

"May I have another? Do I know you well enough to ask?"

"Help yourself," she said coldly.

As he poured out the drink, he said:

"While I was in Brazil this time, I thought a lot about you. Quite seriously, I couldn't stop remembering how absolutely exquisite you looked in your bridal dress and veil, coming up that aisle. It did something to me. I think it made me realise what a fool I'd been to let you go."

She felt her gorge rise. Her whole body seemed like one big flame of indignation and a tension that she could not control.

"I won't listen to you, not if you're going to say things like that."

He shrugged his shoulders.

"Sorry, darling, but I've always been perfectly frank, as you know."

"What's the use—?" she began.

He put out a hand suddenly and touched her cheek.

142

"You really have got the loveliest eyes of any woman I've ever known. Darling, when we were in Rome, if you'd been as cool and remote as you are now, I don't think I'd ever have left you. I might even have married you. But you over-romanticised our association, and I'm not really romantic or chivalrous—like dear Sam. I'm selfish and cruel and a whole lot of other things. But I'm a good artist and I think you'll admit I'm a good lover. I tried to make you see what I was, but you lived in your own dream world. I couldn't measure up to it. I began to feel stifled. You were so much in love with me, Cressida. You made our love affair a bit too honey-sweet. I like a little bitterness, you know that! You were too sensitive—too anxious to involve me."

"All right—perhaps I was—perhaps everything you say is true," she admitted, "but what's the use of dragging it all up now?"

"Because now you could have me on your own terms, isn't that odd, my Little Cat?"

There was an instant's silence. She felt the blood drumming in her ears. She could almost hear the beating of her own heart. It was dreadful, she thought, dreadful to know that she would have given her whole soul to hear him say that when they were in Rome together. In those days, she had been like a creature demented, flinging away principles, honour, everything she once believed in. From the very first moment that he had taken her in his arms and kissed her, she had felt as though she had been struck by lightning. Once, somebody had said in her hearing that lightning could strike twice. But it wasn't true. It certainly would never strike her again.

Dominic came close to her.

"I want to kiss you terribly," he said.

She stepped back.

"Go away, Dominic. Please go away out of this house and don't come back."

He seemed to hesitate. She couldn't have tolerated it if he had, indeed, touched her lips with his. She felt absolutely panic-stricken, but in the whirl of her thoughts, there shone one steadfast light; the thought of Sam and of his blessed healing love.

She looked at Dominic as though he had cast an evil eye

on her and touched her wedding ring as though it were a talisman. Then she started to laugh, hysterically.

"Dominic, you really do amuse me—you can't think how funny you are—how too conceited. Do you imagine you're so fascinating you can just pick up the old threads and expect me to be ready when you chose to pull them? Do you think you can come between Sam and me? You must be mad. Sam and I have only been married a few weeks, and we love each other. I don't love *you* any more. I never will again."

Silence. Dominic was not smiling any more. Cressida fully realised that she had offended him. He could stand argument, anger, criticism—but not ridicule. Few men or women could bear that. Dominic's pride was hurt. She had almost seen him wince while she was talking.

Then he turned away and managed a laugh.

"Glad you find me so amusing, my dear. I must say I asked for it. But it makes no difference to what I feel for you. If you'd rather I didn't stay for dinner, I'll push off, of course. But I think we've both become a little too dramatic, haven't we? My fault, of course, I'd better go before Sam comes in—but I don't promise I won't come back. I find this new relationship of ours rather stimulating and perhaps it'll stop you from turning into a dull, pious little housewife."

"I find that most objectionable!" she began, then stopped, frustrated, fully conscious that she couldn't get rid of Dominic just by being objectionable to *him*, or even by making fun of him. He was much too strong-minded to be diverted from his own purposes in this life. Well, let him do and say what he wanted. She could take it. She just wasn't going to have Sam hurt. With bitter regret, she considered the fact that she had no choice but to go on deceiving Sam. It would be so easy for Dominic to destroy him—through her.

She spoke to Dominic tersely.

"I hear Sam's car now. You'd better stay for supper and let's both try to forget Rome—*please*."

Dominic shrugged his shoulders. Sam came into the house looking, Dominic thought, the worse for wear. He had nothing in common with his glowing and beautiful wife. He was pale and tired and seemed harassed.

"I thought I recognised the Mercedes. Wonderful surprise, old Dom," he began.

"I tried to phone you and tell you I was back in Town, but couldn't get you," said Dominic.

"I've been with my mother. We're running into quite a lot of trouble over her legal affairs. I suppose Cress has told you that poor old Guy had a coronary and Franny is now a widow and a poor one."

"No, I've only just come. I haven't heard much news yet," said Dominic smoothly.

Sam folded his wife in his arms and kissed her.

"Hello, precious—"

"Hello, darling," she replied, but wriggled uncomfortably out of his embrace. She couldn't somehow bear it with Dominic's sardonic, critical gaze upon them. She felt altogether uneasy. The evening was ruined for her even before it began.

Perhaps it was fortunate that Sam was so honest, so trusting, so completely unaware of any atmosphere down here between his wife and his old Cambridge friend.

Cressida left the two men to drink and talk while she hastily relaid dinner in the little dining room, making it three for the meal instead of the expected two.

The rest of the evening was rather a nightmare for her.

Dominic certainly made no reference to the past nor could she accuse him of being anything but coolly friendly and even distant to her. He addressed himself almost exclusively to Sam. They discussed Franny, the financial débâcle, stocks and shares—and politics. Cressida cleared away and stacked the dishes ready for Mrs. Parsloe in the morning, made coffee and brought it into the sitting room. But she continued to feel restless and troubled and far too conscious of Dominic's presence.

The air was fragrant with the aroma of cigars now.

"I've come off rather well. Franny's given me poor Guy's wine cellar and his cabinet of cigars," Sam said with a rueful smile. "Hence the Corona, Dom."

"Very nice, too," said Dominic.

Sam looked at his wife as she poured out the coffee.

"That's a pretty dress, darling. I haven't seen it before."

"It's one of my trousseau ones," she said smiling at him.

"Haven't I got an attractive spouse?"

Sam turned to Dominic, smiling. He had cheered up since dinner. Dominic's presence and conversation had stimulated him and he had lost some of the fatigue and depression he had felt when he had left his mother's house.

Before Dominic could reply, Cressida said hastily:

"Don't embarrass our guest—he may think just the opposite."

Dominic said:

"Oh, not at all, I find your wife most attractive. Incidentally —now I'm back in England, I very much want her to sit for me."

"Splendid idea," said Sam, "You shall be painted, Cress, my darling, and give me the portrait for my birthday present. I've got a birthday in October, haven't I?"

"We'll have to have a few sittings before then," said Dominic easily.

Against her will, Cressida met his dark, mocking gaze.

"I doubt if I'll have time to get up to London," she said.

"Oh, I'll run down and paint you here in your own surroundings."

He spoke with the cool unconcern he had shown since Sam's arrival. But Cressida read something much more in those deep brilliant eyes of his. She felt inexplicably frightened.

"I don't want to be painted—" she began.

"Nonsense, darling," broke in Sam. "Of course you must sit for old Dom. It'll be marvellous if he can capture that elusive Mona-Lisa look of yours."

"You've described your wife exactly," said Dominic.

Cressida sat silent, looking at neither of the men. She felt hot and embarrassed. It was impossible for her not to know what Dominic was thinking. She, too, had to remember the very first painting he had ever done of her. Showing it to her in its initial stages, he had said:

"Your eyes are much bigger, but you have the same shaped face and long neck and La Gioconda's smile. You're a curious mixture, Little Cat—full of warmth and passion and much

146

more generous than La Gioconda could ever have been. But you have her enigmatic look sometimes. It's very intriguing."

Sam said:

"Cress, darling, you've gone all silent. Are you tired?"

"Yes, yes, I'm tired," she said and stood up and looked almost defiantly at Dominic.

"I must push off," he said glancing at his wrist watch. "I've kept you two up too late. It's nearly eleven."

"As late as that," Sam raised his brows, "I'm surprised. The evening has rushed by. I was dog tired when I first got home, but I'm feeling ready for anything now. We ought to all drive up to a night club," he laughed.

"No," said Cressida in an almost sullen voice. "You must get some sleep, Sam. You've had an awful lot to cope with lately and you've got to be up so early."

"I assure you, I'm on my way," said Dominic. "Forgive me for staying so long."

"It hasn't been long enough," said Sam enthusiastically.

Dominic held a hand out to Cressida.

"Good night, and thank you for an excellent dinner."

She refused to meet his gaze. She barely touched his fingers, muttered good night and turned away.

As the two men went out into the drive, she heard Sam's cheerful voice:

"Come down again soon. What about next week-end? I'll make you work in the garden, old Dom. There's still a hell of a lot to do at 'Dorians'—"

She heard Dominic's reply:

"Many thanks. If I won't be a bore, I'd love to come down next week-end."

Slowly Cressida walked up the still uncarpeted stairs to the bedroom which she shared with Sam. Slowly she began to take the cover off the big double bed. To her horror, she found that the tears were gathering in her eyes. They began to drip uncontrollably down her cheeks. When Sam came up he found her lying with her face pressed against the pillow, crying bitterly. Horrified he lay down beside her, trying to caress and comfort her. But when he questioned her, she had no explanation for those tears.

II

ONE warm October evening the Rayes came to dinner at 'Dorians'. It was their second visit, and everybody made a great fuss of Cressida and congratulated her on her cooking, although she had the good sense not to lap up the flattery. She knew that culinary art was not her strong point. However, they had all had a jolly evening and the one thing Freda could genuinely congratulate her daughter upon was her charming and well-kept little house. Cressida obviously took a great pride in it, and she and Sam were always adding some little thing to their collection of treasures. In addition, they now had one or two beautiful pieces of Queen Anne furniture—a tallboy for Sam's room and a tapestry-covered winged chair for the sitting room—both given them by Franny who was fast disposing of her large houseful of furniture. At least that had been left to her as she bitterly told everybody. She had not yet found a small flat, but she would have plenty of stuff to put in it when that day came.

On this night in October, Freda was less happy about her Cressida. She looked much too thin. The mother instinctively felt that all was not as well with her as it should have been. Cressida loved her husband. He was devoted to her, in which case, at the very beginning of their married life, they should have been extremely happy. But neither of them looked a hundred per cent, in Freda's estimation. Cressida seemed to have returned to the difficult girl who had once worried her so much—the uncommunicative, withdrawn Cressida who puzzled her open-hearted, uncomplex mother. Freda had spoken about this once to Cressida's father. He had agreed that he did not think Cressida looked well, but he put Sam's change of demeanour down to all the trouble his mother was causing him.

"That wretched Lady Fennell would be enough to dampen any chap's spirits," was his caustic remark.

Cressida, of course, did not confide in her mother, and Freda refrained from asking intimate questions; although this evening when she first arrived and thought Cressida looked particularly downcast, she had ventured to ask if she felt ill.

"Have you seen a doctor? Is it possible that—"

"No, Mummy, it's not possible," Cressida had broken in sharply. "I'm not ill, and I'm not going to have a baby. I'm just tired."

Freda's rosy face expressed a disappointment that she dare not voice. She did so long for a grandchild. But, of course, she knew that the young things had decided not to have a family quite so soon.

The little party, which was on a Saturday night, included Simon. He was home on an exeat. He was in great form and made a lot of silly jokes. Cressida looked at his freckled face and listened to his giggles and envied her young brother. She had begun to feel quite old and sad and immensely lonely despite the fact that she was Sam's wife; that they shared a double bed and seemed to share so much else. But she was always struggling with that painfully acute conscience of hers; and struggling with *Dominic*. This was wrecking her happiness and playing havoc with her health. She slept badly. Often Sam awoke to find her wide awake. He would take her in his arms and try to soothe and lull her back to her dreams again. She had to pretend, in order to pacify him, that she was all right. But it meant pretending so often that it was getting her down. She simply did not know what to do.

Dominic insisted on coming down at week-ends and each time he was here, she felt more unhappy and confused. She could not deny his devilish charm or his magical ability to interest her and appeal to all that artistic and intellectual side with which Sam, her dear Sam, was not concerned.

Dominic had started to paint her again. Sam insisted that she sat for him and she could not get out of it without appearing too churlish. She could not refuse to invite Dominic for week-ends. Sam was so keen on his coming. She just had to look on helplessly while the two men talked together or worked together in the garden. Dominic proved astonishingly versatile, and not in the least averse to dirtying his beautiful, sensitive hands. He could build a rockery; choose with all an artist's perception, the right kind of flowers to plant, help Sam with odd jobs in the house with equal enthusiasm. Sam continually expressed his gratitude. He told Cressida that old Dom was enormously helpful.

Sometimes, it seemed incredible to Cressida that Sam could not understand how *she* felt. Yet, of course, there was no reason why he *should* guess how miserable, how guilty she felt. As for Dominic, she despised him because he seemed to lack conscience or delicacy of feeling. And she knew that he despised her because she had developed a strong moral sense and regretted Rome.

She was in a terribly invidious position. Often she felt like throwing herself into Sam's arms and pouring out the whole story. The longer she left it, the worse it would be in the long run—she knew that. But what kept her from confession was Sam's affection for his old friend. After every one of Dominic's visits, he praised him more highly.

"Do you know, darling," he had said to Cressida the other night, "old Dom saved my life with his generosity when we were at Cambridge and he is just the same sort of chap now. When he heard that things were going to be so tough for me in the future because of Franny, he offered to lend me money if ever I needed it. Of course, I told him I wouldn't want it, but it was nice of him, you must admit."

Her cheeks hot, Cressida had immediately exclaimed:

"For heaven's sake, don't borrow from Dominic. I'd rather we sold the house and lived in a garret together than we had to borrow from *anybody*."

Sam had stared at her.

"Darling, of course we won't, but why do you always get so het up over Dom? Do you *dislike* him? Everybody else, including Franny, come to that, thinks he's marvellous."

"Well, I don't!" Cressida had wanted to say but had kept her tongue between her teeth. What use to disparage him when she couldn't openly substantiate anything that she said against him; when the whole of her aversion sprang from the dark shadows of the past. Besides, from the very moment that she made Sam feel even faintly that she had no time for

Dominic, she knew he was hurt and disappointed. Entirely for his sake, she went on accepting Dominic.

There was every reason why she should lose weight, and feel tense and nervous. But only *she* knew. She could tell nobody.

She had been quite relieved that Dominic wasn't coming this week-end. He was working with Aldo Canletti again and had gone down to Canletti's house on the river.

"There will be a lot of lovely women there," Dominic had told Cressida. "But nobody who will attract me as you do, my hostile horrid Little Cat."

"Oh, shut up!" she had exclaimed with childish rage.

Yet tonight with a certain horror, she realised that she actually missed him and kept thinking about him. *Oh, Dominic, Dominic, if you would only go away and stay away and let me love Sam in peace,* she kept thinking.

It was good to have her nice parents here and entertain them. Daddy was enjoying the *Nuits St. Georges* that Sam had opened for him—it was his favourite wine. Dear Daddy, Cressida thought with a fond look at her father. How wonderful he was and what an example. Never complaining; helpless invalid though he was. They could carry him in here. They brought his collapsible wheelchair with them in the car and dear Mummy was so pleased he could enjoy these little dinners at 'Dorians'. She watched him with the same affection and pride that she would have given a baby in a high-chair.

But Cressida's heart was very sore every time she glanced at her husband.

If she had changed and lost a lot of her early rapture in their marriage—so had poor Sam. Young and strong though he was, these last few months had been a great strain on him. He looked deadly tired, she thought. Franny went on behaving so unreasonably—making every difficulty she could. Sam had too much to contend with; affairs in the City were very sticky at the moment. She felt for him. She had been quite shocked when, during some discussion about Franny and her debts and moans, Sam had said:

"I think I shall certainly recommend that the words '*At Peace*' should be inscribed on poor old Guy's plaque at Golders Green!"

Cressida had agreed, but it was not like Sam to be so bitter. She was also terribly afraid that she, Cressida, who should have been his greatest comfort, was adding to his burden. Dominic was like a stone wall between them; neither admitted the existence of the barrier, but both were aware that it was there. Slowly but surely, he was creating this rift between them, intangible, but terrifying to Cressida. Sam resented her dislike of his Cambridge friend and thought her unreasonable and unjust. She almost resented the fact that Sam was such a good person. He had idealised her so far that she found it impossible to tell him the truth—disillusion him. It would be like a sword with two edges; with one blow he would lose faith in his wife *and* his friend.

Sometimes Cressida shuddered when she was alone, brooding over it all.

She made the coffee for her guests. Sam and Daddy had finished their talk on politics. Daddy, unfortunately, had noted the half-finished portrait of herself standing up against the bookcase, and now they all discussed it.

"I don't think I like it," Dr. Raye said as he puffed at his pipe. "It isn't somehow my Cress."

"I don't like it either," said Cressida quickly.

"Well, I do," said Sam, "I think it's a masterpiece."

"It's very well painted," put in Freda, cocking her head on one side.

Simon, legs apart, hands in the pockets of his trousers, now grinned at the canvas.

"I think our Cress looks smashing!"

Cressida was wearing that short yellow dress which Sam particularly liked; Dominic had painted her head and shoulders only. The dark, lovely head was thrown back. The lips were slightly parted. The slanting eyes were very green; outstanding, haunting eyes. But it all made Cressida feel sick. She could not forget one moment the other night when Sam had said to Dominic;

"Cress in that portrait might be a little fairy-tale cat that has magically turned into a lovely girl."

Dominic had turned his mocking, laughing gaze on Cressida.

"I think we'll call the portrait *The Little Cat*, shall we?"

Inarticulate, bitterly disliking him, she had turned and walked out of the room.

That, of course, had started another of those unhappy little scenes that all too often took place between Sam and Cressida these days.

"I think you might have been more complimentary to old Dom—he has made a wonderful job of you," Sam complained. "Even if you don't particularly care for him, you must appreciate the chap's work."

"Oh, you're cracked about Dominic," she protested. "I can't think why you don't ask some other of your friends like Tim down here for a change. You can see too much of a person. I'm fed up. You wouldn't like it if I always had the same girl friend down here, would you?"

Sam, as usual, looked hurt and puzzled, then became haughty which, Cressida had discovered, was the usual development in any heated argument with Sam.

"Well, please ask one of your girl friends and I'll tell Dom the spare room is taken," he drawled.

She turned away. Then he caught her arm and pulled her back.

"Oh, Cress, my love, why do we always have to quarrel about old Dom? You really are strange at times. I don't understand you."

"I don't suppose you do," she said in a muffled voice.

"Darling, where is all that lovely love we shared in Majorca?" Sam imprisoned her now with both arms and looked at her with all the old love and longing in his eyes.

" '*Where have all the flowers gone?*' " she quoted and tried to laugh.

"Where indeed," Sam whispered. "I hate these silly battles between us. If you really loathe Dom, I'd better stop asking him down."

"And have you going around at week-ends like a martyr because I've robbed you of your workmate?—no thanks!" she said.

"Now you're being beastly to me," he said in a hurt voice.

She turned to him, buried her face against his chest and hugged him.

153

"I know, I know. Sorry, darling. My nerves are so bad. I really will have to get some tranquillisers."

"Oh, no, you won't! I'm not having my wife reduced to tranquillisers. If Dom gets on your nerves to this extent, I *will* stop asking him at week-ends."

She bit her lip till it hurt, and pressed closer to him.

"No, no, you wouldn't like that. You enjoy his company so much."

"Oh, well, let him finish the portrait and then we'll ease off with the invitations. We can always make an excuse."

Just because he was so nice to her and so anxious to please, Cressida did not take advantage. In a smothered voice, she said:

"Leave things as they are, darling. I expect I'm just being silly. It—it isn't altogether Dominic. We've had rather a wretched start to our married life."

"Well, I'm to blame, of course," said Sam generously. "It's Guy's death and Franny's affairs that have really upset us."

Cressida tried to forget herself and the past. She clasped Sam closer.

"Poor you. You've had an awful time with Franny. It's rotten of me to make things worse for you by being so silly about Dominic. Let's forget him, please, Sam darling. Let's be lovers and forget that we're married."

He laughed, his cheek against her hair.

"That's too cynical. Let's be lovers and *remember* that we're married."

The evening ended happily. Cressida lay in his arms in their big bed. The hunger of their passion was satisfied and they shared a closeness of spirit that seemed to have been eluding them lately. But she still found it difficult to sleep as quickly or as soundly as her husband. She lay awake for a long time listening to the owls hooting to each other down in the woods at the back of their garden; smelling the sweetness of the night-scented stock that drifted through the open windows, as she snuggled warmly against Sam's big strong body. She would make another terrific effort, she told herself, to be sensible about Dominic and not let the past destroy the future.

But that had been two nights ago—before the dinner party with her family.

Coffee had been finished when the telephone bell rang.

Sam half rose, but Cressida shook a hand at him.

"Don't bother, sweetie, I've got to pop upstairs and powder my nose. I'll answer it."

She was feeling quite cheerful in fact when she switched the light on in her bedroom and answered the call. She was really very attached to this room. Lovely chintzes framing the square Georgian windows; and they had 'gone to town' on the pale grey carpet. They had a big yellow bed and a grey and yellow wallpaper. Sam had insisted upon her having one of his best pieces of period furniture for her dressing table; an old walnut spinet. The only thing she was waiting for now was a nice triple mirror.

"Hello," she said as she picked up the telephone receiver and seated herself on the edge of the bed.

Then she heard that low attractive voice which used, in Rome, to make her feel that she wanted to live or to die— according to her mood.

"Little Cat?"

"Oh—it's *you!* Why on earth are you ringing me?" she demanded crossly.

"First week-end I haven't been down for a long time and I miss you."

"Don't be so ridiculous, Dominic."

"I'm bored to death in Aldo's so-called luxury river home. It's full of model girls who either talk too much or can't talk at all. I've eaten too much rich food and drunk too much wine."

"You're drunk now," said Cressida coldly.

"Sober as a judge," came his laughing reply, "but I admit without a judge's legal mind and sense of caution. I know I ought not to be ringing you, but I just wanted to hear my Little Cat's voice. How are you doing without me?"

She felt the colour rise to her cheeks.

"Very nicely thank you. You behave as though I'm not married at all and as though everything between us is exactly as it used to be. You're out of your mind."

"That's how I want it."

"Oh, ring off, and do try to behave sensibly, Dominic. You're crazy."

"It's the sort of craziness you used to find stimulating, my love."

"Well, I don't now," she snapped, although she did not really know whether that was true or not. She was only sure of one thing—her desire to be left in peace to love and live with Sam.

"I hoped you'd answer the phone," she heard him speak again, "I know Sam generally leaves you to do the 'nattering' as he calls it. Where is he?"

"Talking to my mother at the moment. I've got the family here for dinner."

"All cooked by my little no-good chef."

Her eyes sparkled angrily.

"Good-bye—" she began.

She heard a click—then his voice again.

"Don't go, please speak to me. Please tell me you still have some feeling left for me, Little Cat."

"Dominic—" she began to protest, but he cut her short.

"You did love me in Rome, you can't deny it."

"All right, I did."

"Whatever you like to say now, you were mine before you were *his* . . ."

Cressida closed her eyes. She felt something approaching to a sensation of panic. She thought: this is how a moth must feel when it circles blindly around a flame knowing that it will be scorched if it gets one inch nearer. *Oh, damn Dominic! Damn him!*

With all the sincerity of her nature, she wanted to be faithful in mind as well as body to the man she had married. It was killing her—this terrible, remorseless effort Dominic seemed to be making to pull her back into the fire. How selfish he was! Out of that gross egotism, he was willing to betray his oldest friend and ruin her marriage.

"Oh, God, Dominic, why don't you leave me alone!" she said in a choked voice.

"Are you weakening, my darling? Are those gorgeous green eyes of yours softening a little? Do you remember the nude I painted of you lying on my couch? You looked like Goya's study of The Maja Unclothed. You both had the same dark hair spread against the cushions, and that languorous, enticing expression."

There was another click. And suddenly the panic in Cressida's mind crystallised into a definite fear. *There was somebody else on the line.* It flashed through her brain for a scalding second that *somebody*—maybe even Sam himself—had picked the receiver up down in the hall, heard Dominic's voice and decided to cut in to the conversation.

"Cressida—" began Dominic.

"Good-bye," she said breathlessly and put down the receiver.

For an instant, she sat breathing rapidly, staring vacantly into space. Then she pulled herself together. She could hear her young brother calling:

"Cress—I say—Cress, do come on down. Daddy's feeling tired and Mum wants us to go home."

She ran downstairs.

Her fascinated gaze was drawn immediately to her husband's face. He did not look at her. She could not even see the expression in his eyes because he was talking to her mother and they had already lifted the doctor into the wheelchair and Sam was pushing him to the front door.

Freda embraced her daughter, and thanked her warmly for the dinner. It was lovely, she declared. They had adored it. She thought Cressida's cooking had improved, but her father got tired quickly and she could see he wanted to get back.

"Yes, of course," said Cressida.

There were good-night kisses all round. Sam stood out in the darkness for a moment after his mother-in-law had driven away. Cressida, nervously watching, saw him light a cigarette. Then he said:

"If you don't mind, I'm going for a short walk."

Her heart began to thud. She knew even before he spoke that her worst fears were justified.

Sam *had* picked up that telephone downstairs, and listened —possibly because he had something to say to Old Dom. Sam must have also heard that last damning bit about the 'nude' and that bit when Dominic had reminded her that she had been *his* before she was Sam's.

For a ghastly second, Cressida tried to keep up appearances.

"It is rather a lovely night for a walk. Shall I come with you, darling?"

"No, thank you," said Sam.

Never had he spoken to her in such an icy stilted voice. It froze her. She stood there feeling faint and sick. He shut the front door between them.

12

HE was out such a long time that Cressida began to feel desperately anxious. Sam was a sensible, placid type of man. Surely he wouldn't behave like a neurotic—a weakling who when crushed by this sort of blow would buckle under it? But her sense of guilt was enormous. It defeated her normal powers of reasoning. Besides, she didn't know how much he had heard. That, most of all, was what disturbed her. She couldn't straighten things out at all. She didn't know how he really felt about her. She wanted to go to bed because she was tired, but she couldn't even bring herself to go upstairs and run her bath.

She walked up and down the sitting room—out into the garden—into the house again.

She had never longed more to see Sam—to find herself back in the days of their early love when she had felt that Rome was way behind her and that she had a right to accept Sam's love. When she used to be able to answer the tremendous devotion in his eyes with generous, contented love shining in her own.

She was a nervous wreck by the end of the second hour of waiting like this, alone, for Sam to come home.

Inevitably she remembered how Dominic teased her about her name.

Cressida the Unfaithful, he had said, mocking her.

She put her face in her hand and giggled hysterically, but the giggle gave way to tears.

I didn't want to be unfaithful to Sam—I haven't really been . . . It all took place before I married Sam.

But it was the lie that counted with him—that, she knew. The pretence over Dominic.

Then Sam walked into the house.

She had just gone upstairs when she heard the front door shut. She turned and rushed down again. She stood on the last step of the staircase, looking at him, uncertainly.

His face betrayed nothing to her. He seemed placid—even indifferent.

"Not in bed yet?" he asked coolly.

She gave a shaky laugh.

"No—I couldn't . . . I didn't want . . . I mean . . . I waited up for you," she stammered.

"You shouldn't have bothered."

Terror seized her.

"Sam—" she began, all her nerves jumping and her body tense, but he interrupted:

"I can see you want a showdown. Well, I don't."

Her sense of terror increased.

"But Sam—we've got to talk this thing over. I can see you . . . you've changed . . . you're upset with me . . . oh, I suppose you heard what Dominic said on the phone!"

Now he looked at her with a glance that struck her as being almost contemptuous and it was like a knife piercing the depths of her heart.

"Yes, I listened in. Not very noble of me, was it? I'm not by nature a chap who listens in, or eavesdrops behind doors. But I picked up the receiver and I wondered who it was because you'd been on the phone some time. Just natural wonder. No suspicion. I'm not a suspicious chap. I didn't realise you were talking to Dominic. Then I heard . . . Oh, let's not talk about it, *please*," he ended abruptly.

She went up to him and gripped both his arms.

It was the first time she had ever heard him call Dominic by his full name. It seemed to her that in one fell swoop 'old Dom' was finished—the whole friendship was washed up. It was almost more than she could bear, because behind Sam's apparent coolness there must lie an infinity of pain.

"Please let me talk to you. Let me tell you—" she began.

Again he interrupted:

"I couldn't face it tonight. Sorry."

"Surely you can't want to got to bed—surely you couldn't sleep before we have talked things over."

"What is there to talk about?" he asked.

She gasped.

"Sam!"

"If you're worried as to what I heard, I'll tell you. I know now you belonged to Dominic before me. That you had a hot affair with him in Rome and that he painted you in the nude. Also that he still loves you."

She felt the sweat pouring down her back. Her teeth were chattering.

"Sam," she said. "I can't stand it if you talk to me like this."

"I didn't think I could stand what I heard, either. But I've realised, while I've been out walking these last two hours, that one can stand anything. It's just a question of getting over the initial shock. I've never been a dramatic sort of person, as you know. I dare say Dominic Miln could hurl himself around the stage and play a sensational role begging you for details, accusing you of this and that, telling you that he wanted to commit suicide . . . etc. etc. That's maybe how you'd like me to behave, but I can't. I just want to be left alone. I need time to recover my equilibrium."

He looked straight at Cressida now. She looked back. The condemnation in his gaze hurt her more acutely than anger could have done. She was seeing a new side to the man she had married and rather a frightening one. Later in a quiet moment, she remembered with a new respect and admiration his self-control. But tonight his attitude roused nothing in her but consuming fear and the awfulness of not knowing what he meant to do. Of course, he couldn't do much, she argued to herself, except pack and leave her. She *hadn't* been unfaithful to him. He couldn't really condemn her for what she *had* done in Rome.

Her mind went back to the evening in Majorca when they had suddenly found themselves concerned with the young Italian from Palma who had murdered his bride-to-be. She remembered asking Sam what he would have done in a similar case. His answer had been: '*I expect I'd be bloody angry*'. But he had also said that a man never knew what he would do in certain circumstances until he was actually faced with them.

Then he had ended by telling her that it would be the deceit he'd dislike rather than what the girl had done in the past.

She clutched his arm again.

"All right, we won't discuss things tonight, but I do want

you to know one thing—you must let me say this, Sam—whatever happened in Rome, I don't love Dominic *now*. I *don't*! I love *you*!"

She fancied his lips relaxed a little, but he drew gently away from her fingers.

"Thank you," he said with an obliterating courtesy, "I'll try to remember that."

Then as he began to walk away from her, he looked over his shoulder, and added:

"*If* I can believe you."

That meant final defeat and humiliation for Cressida. Completely crushed, she watched him go up the stairs.

He called from the upper landing:

"You might bolt the front door, and I think we left the french windows open."

"I'll see to it," she called back, she found it a tremendous effort to get the words out.

But she took some small comfort in attending to the menial tasks they performed every evening. She even brought herself to go into the kitchen and lay their breakfast. Sam never ate a cooked breakfast during the week before he rushed to the station, but on a Sunday morning, he enjoyed his bacon and eggs. Usually he cooked them himself, and took her tray up to her in bed, which he called 'her sabbath treat'.

He was so kind—such a dear. Oh God, she thought, if only I'd been frank with him from the very start.

And now, bitterly, she thought of those words 'lightning strikes twice'. It had struck her in Rome—a terrible blinding light that had hurled her into Dominic's arms. Now it was striking again—and this time the lightning was utterly destructive. It seemed to her that all three of them would be annihilated by it. But it didn't seem to matter about Dominic. *Nor* herself. It was only Sam. All the way along she had behaved as she had done because she had wanted to spare him.

Her anguish of mind increased when she found Sam already in the big bed they had shared with such passion and contentment since they came to live at 'Dorians'; in bed, and asleep. Pretending to be asleep perhaps, but he had his back turned to her and he did not speak to her when she came into the room.

She turned off the light. In utter misery she undressed in the dark, then got into bed with him.

He made no effort to touch her. After a moment she even heard his deep, regular breathing and realised that he *was* fast asleep.

Resentment took the place of her fear, although misery remained uttermost. But she lay wide awake with the hot tears rolling down her cheeks, smothering her sobs, and wondering indignantly how he could possibly have gone to sleep like this. How like a man! No matter what happened he could still eat and sleep. Men must, she thought bitterly, be very differently constructed from women; and much less sensitive. How *could* Sam, knowing what he did, feeling how he did, drop asleep just like that? Of course, he was probably very tired. He had been digging the herbaceous border all morning and he had had a tough week what with the Stock Exchange and Franny. Everybody had said tonight that he looked very tired. She tried to excuse him, but couldn't altogether. He had been right when he had said she wanted a showdown; so she did. She couldn't tolerate this awful tension, this atmosphere between them. She found that she was forced to tolerate it. Sam continued to sleep.

Only once he woke. She hadn't yet closed her eyes. He turned toward her, flung out an arm and for an agonising moment she believed that he meant to draw her against him. But as his hand touched her breast, he seemed to wake fully and at once drew away and turned on his other side again.

"Sorry," he muttered.

"Oh Sam," she whispered desolately, "*please*! . . ."

But she stopped. He neither moved nor spoke again.

She buried her face in the pillow.

She must have fallen asleep herself soon after that because when she woke, Sam was no longer beside her. The sun was streaming through the window. It was going to be another lovely day. The sort of Sunday they always hoped for.

She put on her dressing gown and slippers and ran downstairs. She found a note on the kitchen table which at once struck fresh misery and fear at her heart. It was from Sam.

It said:

"*Cress, I've got a lot to think about and please forgive me if I don't enter into a detailed discussion with you just yet. I can't. I've got to get myself sorted out. It's been a pretty heavy blow. You and my best friend.*

I've gone up to Town. Hope you don't mind. I've taken the car, but I'm going to spend the day with Franny. There are still a lot of accounts to be sorted out for her. It seemed a good idea. Needless to say, I shall not let her know what has happened.

I'll be back later this evening. Sam."

Cressida crumpled the note and threw it into the bin. Her cheeks were red and her lips trembling. She was in tears again. She felt quite sick. The whole of her marriage seemed to have crashed about her. All the carefree, gorgeous happiness had gone. Even though her conscience—and Dominic—had troubled her these last few weeks, it had been bearable because Sam didn't know about it. They had had a lot of fun together. She had basked in his love. It was too awful now to think that he didn't love her any more, which must be the case, she considered, or he wouldn't be treating her like this. He wouldn't even give her a chance to talk to him. He just drew his own conclusions. Well, they must be very bad. She couldn't really be surprised. But she did think he was being rather cruel. He was proud. His faith must have taken a frightful belting, but couldn't he have been a bit more understanding ? She had always imagined that Sam of all men was tolerant.

Maybe it was because he had loved her so much that he didn't find it too easy to be so. And if Dominic hadn't been the man, it would, perhaps have been better. Everything was made worse because old Dom had been his Best Man and his best friend, *and* her secret lover.

Cressida went through a bad hour or two after reading Sam's note.

'Dorians' seemed horribly quiet. She felt deserted. She even began to feel angry with Sam for treating her like this. She kept changing her mind; first of all, she told herself that she deserved all that she got. Then she mentally accused Sam of cruelty and injustice in running away from the showdown just because *he* didn't want one. What about having some concern for what *she* wanted? He must realise how terrible *she* felt about it all.

She brewed herself a cup of strong coffee, but ate nothing. After making the bed and dusting the rooms, she stood out in the garden and smoked a cigarette and tried to make up her mind what to do.

The day was going to seem terribly long.

She thought of Dominic, probably enjoying himself on the river with Aldo and his girls. She thought of his unscrupulous attitude towards the whole affair. *She hated him.* He had wrecked her life. How would *he* feel when he knew that Sam had found out? She was quite sure he would be genuinely sorry. He would hate not to be able to come down here any more and work in the garden or the house with Sam. He wouldn't like losing Sam's friendship and respect. Dominic, of course, wanted to have his cake and eat it; he was the sort always to take—rarely to give.

A dozen times that day she was on the verge of telephoning her mother-in-law's house and begging Sam to come home because she couldn't stand being alone any more. But she didn't. She couldn't, somehow, behave without any pride. Sam wasn't the only one to be proud. Several times, too, she thought of telephoning her mother and asking her to come and talk the whole thing out, but she couldn't do that, either. She had never confided in Freda, sweet and nice though she was. She just *couldn't*. And there wasn't a single friend to whom she would have told *this* unhappy story.

What then was going to happen, Cressida kept asking herself. Did Sam intend just to go on living with her in a state of hostility? Would he never forgive her? Did he think that what she had done deserved perpetual punishment?

She began to work herself up into a state of fresh resentment against him because he had rushed up to Franny and left her, his wife, to face this awful day alone. Neither could she forgive him because he had behaved so heartlessly last night and slept while she lay crying.

"All men are beastly. I hate them all!" she began to sob to herself as she turned the thing over and over again in her mind. Sam had failed her. Yes, when she had needed him most, he had failed her. So she had something to forgive *him*. Heavens, what had she done, choosing two such men; one was too bad, and the other too good. Why did everybody have to be so extreme?

But all these reflections ended in tears and self-reproach again, for Cressida knew that there could be small excuse for her not telling Sam the truth in the first place.

The only thing she could do was to hope nobody would call at 'Dorians' today and create a difficulty for her in having to explain her husband's absence on a Sunday.

It seemed to make things all the worse because it was such a glorious day. The sun never stopped shining. She thought miserably of Sam wasting this lovely weather with Franny, having to stay cooped up in the house listening to her petty grievances.

When did he mean to come home? She watched the clock. She had spent a little time in the garden weeding one of the beds that they were preparing for the spring. At six o'clock she started to watch the drive, hoping every moment to see Sam and the Triumph Herald.

She began to sulk.

He might have rung me. He might show some interest as to whether I'm alive or dead, she thought sullenly.

Freda had rung up during the morning to thank her for the dinner party. Cressida had to be bright and breezy with her, but dissolved into tears once she put down the receiver. Freda had said, at the end of their conversation:

"It's such a joy to your father and me to see you so happily married, dear."

Cressida bit on those words for some time afterwards. Surely Sam, if he really loved her as much as he had always said he did, wouldn't want to put a complete end to their old happy relationship?

She swerved from dark despair to forlorn hope. She had spent an hour cleaning all the silver that Franny had unearthed from a family chest and given them.

She then rather pathetically decided to make an apple pie for Sam's supper. He *must* come home for supper and he had a great weakness for apple pie. He had complimented her because she had learned to make such light short pastry. Down at the bottom of the garden there were some old but fecund apple trees. She went down, picked a basketful of fruit and made her pie. She was just taking it out of the oven —about seven o'clock—when she heard car wheels.

She looked quickly into the little mirror she had hung in the kitchen. All day she knew she had been a sight. Eyes red-rimmed. No colour at all. Hastily she dived into the bag that was on the kitchen table, found a lipstick and outlined her lips. Then taking off her overall, she ran through the hall to meet her husband. At least, she thought, she had on something that Sam liked her in—turquoise cotton slacks and a sleeveless shirt to match which she used to wear on their honeymoon.

Then, to her disappointment and dismay, she saw the big Mercedes—and Dominic—outside the front door.

When Cressida saw Dominic, her spirits sank so low that she felt they could fall no further. This was *it*, she thought. *Now it only remains for Sam to turn up which he surely will and the whole boat will sink.*

Dominic, knowing nothing of what had happened, seemed in good spirits. He approached her with his customary slow graceful tread, wiping face and neck with a silk handkerchief. "Warm this evening—a bit thundery I think now the sun has gone in," he began cheerfully. Then he stopped. He saw the expression on Cressida's face and his smile faded. "Anything wrong? You look upset, my dear—"

"I am," she broke in grimly. And now she turned away and walked into the house knowing that he would follow. The last few hours had been so terrible to her she had not noticed the weather, but true enough, the sky was rapidly darkening, a storm was approaching (all round, she thought ironically). A few heavy raindrops began to fall. From the distance came the first low growl of thunder. She could hear the strange shrill warning call from a pheasant down in the spinney. It always did have an ominous sound, she considered.

She faced Dominic in the sitting room. Her voice was quite steady as she spoke to him although her hands trembled, clasped like a schoolgirl's behind her back.

"Well—thanks to your ghastly indiscretion last night, it's all over," she said.

He stared at her genuinely uncomprehending.

"What's over?"

"What have you come here for this evening?" she cut in, ignoring his question. She spoke rather rudely. She knew it. She knew, too, that she did not care one jot about Dominic Miln any more. The one-time god had been deprived of the last little coat of glory in her eyes. He might still be the handsome, rich, interesting artist, with his Brazilian blood and his brilliant brain. Tonight she saw him through eyes no longer blind. She saw him as he was—a base, sensual, utterly selfish person, as the weapon that had wounded Sam and threatened their happiness.

"I hate you," she said between her teeth. "I can't tell you how much I hate you."

He stared at her, then smiled and shrugged:

"Darling Cress, I really don't know what all this is about. Where's Sam?"

"On his way down from town—he'll be back any moment and if you don't mind, I'd rather you weren't here when he turns up."

"What's he doing in town on a Sunday? I took it for granted you were both here as usual, and old Sam would be busy with his week-end gardening."

"You take too much for granted," Cressida said. "Why did you come down without an invitation, anyhow?"

It was his turn to colour.

"You're being most unusually impolite, my darling."

"I am *not* your darling."

"Now, look, let's cut out this dialogue. It's too boring. I came down because Aldo and his friends *were* boring, and I missed you—and even Sam." Dominic gave that sudden, rather engaging, smile which used to tear her heart in two. "So—" he went on, "I decided to come along as fast as the Merc would bring me and spend the evening with you. Of course, if you don't want me, my dearest—"

Cressida broke in:

"Listen, Dominic. You said all kinds of ghastly, dangerous

things to me on the phone last night. You must have been quite insane. I was in my bedroom, but Sam picked up the phone downstairs and heard what you said."

Now Dominic changed colour. He looked startled.

"What *did* I say, actually?"

"Doubtless you don't remember," she sneered. "You never did remember half the things you said in the old days. They didn't seem important to *you*. But last night it was. Sam now knows that you and I—you and I—" She stumbled over the words and added miserably, "Oh, *God*!"

Dominic sat down. He pulled the usual packet of cigarettes from his coat pocket and a box of matches which he shook automatically.

"God," he echoed. "So that's it."

"Yes, that's it."

"How much did he hear? What did he say to you?"

"Nothing much. He refused to have a showdown last night. He said he couldn't take it until he had sorted himself out."

"But he must have said *something*."

"He just intimated that he had listened in. He didn't mean to. He's always rather inquisitive, Sam, and he just wanted to know who I was talking to, and when he heard your voice, he decided to stay and put in a word. A nice affectionate word!" she ended with a sad, ironic laugh.

"That's all you know?"

"It's enough. He neither touched me nor spoke to me all night and in the morning when I woke up, he'd already gone up to his mother and left a note saying he'd be back this evening. I just *don't* want him to find you here. You've done enough harm."

Dominic stood up, a cigarette between his lips, hands in his pockets, and began to walk up and down, up and down, scowling as the smoke stung his eyes.

"Oh, *hell*," he muttered. "I must say this is unexpected. It was silly of me. I'd had too much champagne. You told me I was drunk. I was. They say that when a man has had too much to drink, he has fewer inhibitions and I rather let myself go, talking to you. Obviously if I'd thought twice, I wouldn't have said so many intimate, incriminating things."

"Well, you've said them and the harm's done."

"He can't take us to the Divorce Court for an infidelity committed before he ever met you," said Dominic, spreading out a hand. "It really is rather ridiculous."

Cressida felt angry and resentful—the two emotions which seemed, these days, to predominate over all others when she was with Dominic. How terrible, she thought, that one could love a man as she had once loved this one, then grow to despise him. His world—that world of art, amoral living, 'moonshine', had once been the world she wanted. Now she needed something more solid and comforting. She realised how murderous life could have been, married to Dominic. With everything perpetually unhappy and tense. He was attractive —who could deny it? She could not even now—for all her newly-developed hostility.

He threw away his cigarette end, came up, and put both hands on her shoulders:

"Little Cat, I'm sorry. Please believe I wouldn't have had this happen. I'm really quite attached to Sam. You may not believe me, but I've no wish to hurt him and I didn't want him to find out about us—not in this sort of way, anyhow. I can realise how it's hit you both. I *am* sorry. Please believe me!"

She backed away from him. If he had gone on shrugging his shoulders and sneering, she would have found it easier to cope with him. She didn't want him to be nice and understanding for when he looked down at her so contritely, spoke so remorsefully, she felt the hatred within her dissolving. She knew that she was partly to blame for the whole thing.

Her happiness with Sam was in mortal danger. She wanted desperately to get back to the safety and love in her life with him. She couldn't bear to feel it slipping away.

Two big, burning tears welled into her eyes and ran down her cheeks.

"Oh, Dominic, what are we going to do? I'm so frightened."

He turned uncomfortably from the sight of those tears. They made him feel guilty, which was a thing Dominic Miln had hardly ever done in his life. He'd always found some smooth way of passing his share of guilt on to the next person. Not very commendable and he knew it. It had been the same in Rome—he had pretended to himself that he could sneak out of Cressida's life without scruple or compassion because he had warned her that he might do so. But, in fact, her complete love and trust in him had deserved more consideration. Sam's friendly confidence, dating back from their Cambridge days, that deserved something more, too.

"Oh, God, you make me feel frightful!" he said. "I really am sorry. Would it make things any better if I tell you that I think it's because I really and truly have grown to love you, as well as *want* you, that all this happened? I'd be ready if you said the word to take you away and marry you, if Sam will divorce you."

Cressida stared at him incredulously. Her tears gave way to the unhappiest laughter he had ever heard.

"Oh, oh!" she exclaimed, "What a thing! If you'd asked me in Rome, I'd have just about died of happiness. Now I find it funny."

"I didn't know I was a humorist," he said coldly.

"Dominic, I didn't mean to be too beastly," she relented. "I know I ought to thank you for offering to make a dishonest woman of me all over again—then to marry me. But it does seem a bit strange—coming from you of all people, who always said the very word marriage terrified you. I don't believe that you love me now and even if I did, I wouldn't want to go away with you. I certainly don't *love you* any more."

He shrugged his shoulders in his graceful fashion. His lips curled.

"Straight from the shoulder. O.K. I've had it. I suppose the best thing I can do now is to go away and stay away."

She looked at him with eyes that were blind with tears again.

"Yes—I think that would be best."

"I'll get my portfolio," he said, and walked across the room and picked it up. "Keep the painting of yourself. It's only half-finished, but it isn't bad even as it is."

She made no answer. Once she had loved him so very much. It all seemed so sad that it should have ended in this ugly way.

Lightning suddenly flashed, illuminating the whole room and both their faces as they stared at each other. It was followed by a crack of thunder. Then down came the rain, beating noisily against the windows. The storm had broken.

She forced herself to say:

"You'd better wait until this is over, hadn't you?"

"No," he said, "I don't mind driving in a storm and I'm sure you won't worry about me."

"Oh, please . . ." she began to protest.

He answered, but she didn't hear what he said because there was another lightning flash and peal of thunder. The storm seemed to be breaking with great speed and violence.

From the doorway, Dominic turned and looked at her.

"I'm not trying to run out on you and I'm not in the least afraid of facing Sam. In fact, I would have liked to have done so, but you seem to think it's better for him not to find me here tonight."

She nodded.

Suddenly he ran back and caught and held her close.

"Oh, Little Cat—my darling Little Cat! I'm so sorry. I seem to have hurt you twice in this life. I feel ghastly about it. I've behaved so badly and I know it. But I did think we might have settled down to a beautifully triangular friendship. Lots of people do, but I realise now that you aren't the type to have two men in your life, and old Sam is a complete idealist. He couldn't stand up to discovering you were only human. He prefers his angel. I can imagine that what he now knows about us must seem like complete disaster. But I am sure he'll get over it. He's devoted to you. I'm going to miss you both, enormously; I feel rather like a chap who's turned himself out of Paradise. If you want to know!"

At first she had stayed motionless unbending in his embrace, but suddenly her whole body relaxed and she hid her face against his shoulder. Great gasping sobs shook her.

She said:

"Oh, Dominic, Dominic, please go—please!"

He released her. She flung herself on the sofa and cried like a heartbroken child. But she knew that the tears were not because of Dominic's departure, but because, between them, they had hurt Sam.

13

AFTER the big white Mercedes Benz had roared away into a downpour of rain, the storm seemed to pass as suddenly and violently as it had come. The thunder growled on in the distance.

Cressida stopped crying, went upstairs and dabbed her wet burning face with witch hazel. She tried to make her face up ready for Sam, but decided mournfully that her eyes were so swollen, she could do little to produce any glamour; so she gave it up and went downstairs again.

It was now almost dark and much colder. She fetched a cardigan. She was shivering, partly with nerves, and because she hadn't eaten a thing today. She had never felt so ill or so unhappy.

She opened the front door and stared out. The garden was drenched. Rain was still falling gently. The sky was torn with ragged clouds that were fast dispelling. She noticed that the mowing machine had been left out and thought how annoyed Sam would be because he hadn't put it away.

She closed the front door and went back into the house and into the kitchen. Looking at the clock, her sorrow gave way to a very definite anxiety.

It was nine o'clock. *Nine* and Sam not back! Surely he had meant to come home for supper. She couldn't understand it.

Suddenly she decided to telephone her mother-in-law's house. She must speak to Sam. She must establish contact between them or go mad.

Coot, Franny's new companion, answered the phone.

"Oh, hello, Coot," said Cressida, trying to speak in her ordinary way. "How are you?"

"All the better for having had dear Sam with us all day. It was sweet of you to let him come up. Darling Franny really couldn't cope alone. I am very good with a lot of things, but we needed Sam to go through all those financial papers. Poor Guy left such a pile."

"Sam still there?" asked Cressida, her heart knocking.

"Why, no, dear. He left ages ago."

Cressida drew the back of her hand across her dry lips.

"When, Coot?"

"Oh, it must have been about half past six. He said he knew there'd be a lot of traffic at this time and he wanted to be home for supper. He should have been with you about eight, shouldn't he?"

Cressida worked frantically in her mind to think of a suitable explanation of this. Whatever happened she mustn't let Coot see—or repeat to Franny—that she was worried about Sam. So she created a gallant lie.

"*I* know what he's done. He said the next time he came down from Town he might stop and see a client who lives in Reigate. We always go back through Reigate. I'm sure that's what happened."

"And of course there's been that dreadful storm, did you have it?" asked Coot.

"Yes. He's probably still in Reigate, waiting for it to clear. How's Franny?"

"A little better, I think, but still very depressed, poor darling."

When Cressida put the telephone receiver down, having been forced into a lengthy talk with her mother-in-law who had grabbed the receiver—she started to worry again. Franny, of course, had talked about nothing but herself and all the things that she wasn't going to be able to afford. At least Cressida gathered that Sam had not so much as breathed a word about *them*. She might have known. He was so loyal. The only information she gained was that Coot had said before she handed Cressida over to Franny, that they thought Sam looked very exhausted.

If it were only mere exhaustion, Cressida thought with deep melancholy. But she could well believe that Sam had been thinking about her all day—and Dominic. Feeling things dreadfully. Perhaps he had even begun to hate her. Perhaps that was why he hadn't come home. Unless, of course, he had had an accident. The roads couldn't be very good after that storm; although Sam never drove terribly fast.

She began to be frantically worried now. She felt so faint and nauseated that after another half hour passed she made herself a cup of strong coffee and nibbled at a cheese biscuit. She looked mournfully at the supper laid on the kitchen table. She wished so much that Sam was with her—that it was like all the other Sundays when they happily ate their meal, and shared love and laughter together.

She returned to the sitting room, torn with the strain, she picked up the canvas that Dominic had left there. His legacy to them. She stared at her painted face, then dropped the canvas on to the floor again.

Tomorrow she would burn it, or throw it into the dustbin. She didn't want to keep any record of Dominic. She wanted to erase him entirely from her life, and most of all to forget *Rome*.

But how would Sam feel about things? Would he want to go on living with her? Surely he couldn't be so prudish and Victorian that he would punish her like that for her deception? That wouldn't be in keeping with his natural kindliness and generosity.

Cressida was in a bad state by the time she heard the Triumph Herald pull up outside the front door. She rushed to the door, mad with relief, and opened it. The rain had stopped. There were even a few stars out in the sky. The air was full of the scent of stocks and wet grass and the strong odour of drenched earth.

She watched Sam get out of the car and walk slowly towards her. Anxiously she peered through the darkness. As he came into the hall and the light fell on his face, she was appalled to see how haggard he looked. Haggard, and quite changed. Not a smile. He just *looked* at her.

"Oh, Sam—you're terribly late—" she began to stammer.

"Yes," he said.

"I rang your mother half an hour ago. Coot said you left them at half past six."

"Yes," he repeated.

He walked past her into the sitting room. She followed. He seated himself on the sofa and locked his hands together. She looked down at him. His whole attitude was one of immense fatigue. His eyes were rimmed with red.

"Oh, Sam," she said again, her voice a little hoarse. "I've been dreadfully upset and worried all day. I've been nearly out of my mind—honestly I have! It's been too grim."

He glanced up at her silently. At least, she decided, his eyes were not as angry or hostile as they had been last night. They were just full of an immeasurable sadness that hurt her even more than his anger could have done.

She found his continued silence alarming and quite unbearable. There was no room in her mind for pride. She felt nothing but a desire to humble herself and plead for his forgiveness—as much for his sake as for her own. Anything, *anything* to drive the awful sadness out of the blue fine eyes that were usually so full of shining happiness and good faith.

She flung herself on her knees beside him and encircled one of his legs with both her arms. She laid her cheek against his knee.

"Sam, please, *please* forgive me. I've been so terribly unhappy all day. Sam, I couldn't bear it when I woke up and found you'd gone away. All day I've been imagining what it would be like to live without you. I couldn't bear it last night, either, when you wouldn't speak to me or touch me. Oh, Sam, do you hate me so much for what I did? I hadn't met you then and I wanted dozens of times to tell you about Dominic, but when I found you liked him so much it made it all so difficult. I couldn't bear to disillusion you in both of us. Can't you believe that I do love you now and that Dominic doesn't mean a row of pins to me?"

She raised her head as she asked this last question, looking at him distractedly.

Then he said:

"Dominic won't mean a row of pins to anyone any more. He's dead."

Terror gripped her.

"Oh, my God, what do you mean?"

"Sorry to break it so abruptly. The reason why I'm late is because when I got to that bend in the road—there's a double white line actually—just before you come into Merstham—I was held up in a queue. Not a very big one. Most of the traffic was coming the other way from Brighton being a

Sunday night. But I could see there had been an accident. Some damn fool, so I thought, had tried to pass in spite of the double line. It was pouring and I suppose the lights were a bit dazzling, and there it was. There were three cars involved and the wreckage was strewn across the road, plus police cars and so forth. Another chap and I got out and walked up to see if we could do anything. It was then that I saw and recognised the white Mercedes."

"Oh, my God!" repeated Cressida, utterly shaken.

"Dominic was lying on the road wrapped in a blanket with an A.A. patrolman kneeling beside him," continued Sam in a slow, heavy voice. "I could see his face—rather badly cut. They were bandaging him. I suppose I didn't think of anything then except that he was my old friend and I told the police so. I kneeled down and spoke to Dominic. He opened his eyes and looked at me and then—then he died. That's all."

"That's all? He just died—like that?" her face was colourless.

"Yes. They said he had internal injuries. It was from shock, too. A man in one of the cars involved—who wasn't actually hurt—told me that Dominic was driving like a maniac. It was obviously the heavy rain and the dazzle of lights and going over that double line that caused the smash. It was sheer suicide, although I doubt very much if Dominic *meant* to have an accident. He wasn't the sort of man to want to die that way, was he?"

Cressida shook her head. She knelt there, dumbfounded, shaking, clutching Sam's leg.

"And he—didn't speak at all?" she whispered the question.

"Yes, in fact, he said two things. '*Sorry, old boy*' and '*Don't be a damned fool and hold it against poor Cress.*'"

That broke Cressida. She sat back on her haunches and covered her face with her hands.

It seemed that Sam could still not bring himself to touch her. He got up and walked the other side of the room. She heard his voice.

"There wasn't anything I could do after that, so I just told the police who he was and gave them Aldo Canletti's address.

He'll know who to contact in Brazil. I believe Dominic has an uncle there."

Sam spoke so quietly, so steadily; he seemed so calm in spite of the terrible thing he had just seen—it helped to restore some of Cressida's composure. She got on to her own feet. Her eyes were dry, stinging. She was deeply shocked. But she couldn't cry. She couldn't cry even for Dominic. It was all too sudden. It seemed only a few moments ago that Dominic had been here, laughing at her with those brilliant, mocking eyes—using the old pet name:

"Little Cat!"

"What an awful, awful thing to happen," she said in a smothered voice.

"Yes," said Sam. "And it's odd how one's feelings—one's whole attitude towards a person—can change in a few moments. I've never wanted to commit a murder, but I really think I would have willingly killed Dominic just before I caught up with that accident. He'd done such a lot of harm— to you—to me—to both of us. Then I saw him lying there dying, and I didn't hate him at all. It was just my friend, old Dom, lying there, dying. It shook me."

"Sam," said Cressida, "I've all kinds of things that I was going to say to you, ready and waiting for when you got home tonight. But that was when *he* was alive. Now he's dead, I suppose it does make a difference."

"Yes," said Sam.

"I know what you're like, Sam," she was shivering. "You just said yourself that you could only think of him as the old friend you were so fond of when you found him dying. You admit you don't hate him any more. But I suppose you still hate me?"

Now he looked at her with clear direct gaze.

"No, I could never hate you, Cressida."

"Then you don't love me any more."

He hesitated, then said:

"I can't answer for myself tonight. I'm in such a state. I'd far rather not discuss it till tomorrow."

Now she gave an hysterical laugh.

"Well, if you think I'm going through another night like

last night, you're wrong. I know men are different from women. *You* could go to sleep. I couldn't. Not for hours and hours. I was absolutely crazy with misery. You were controlled and hard and *different*. I could never have believed you'd be like that," she added in a choked voice.

Sam sat down as though his legs were too tired to support him. He locked his fingers together.

"I don't think you quite understand what all this has meant to me."

She looked at him in sudden bitterness. Before he came home, she had been full of tremendous remorse, so wildly anxious to restore the old relationship between them that she had been ready to efface herself—say anything—do anything —so long as he would forgive her. Now, she resented *his* attitude. Quite apart from the shock of knowing that Dominic had driven away from this house to his death only a few hours ago—she began to feel that Sam was behaving rather inhumanly. He, whom she once thought the most kindly man on earth.

She broke out:

"Oh, I know how good you are—how terribly decent— how incapable of behaving like *Dominic*. I know that I had no right to marry you without telling you I'd lived with him in Rome, either. But I thought the whole thing was behind me. I also thought that what took place before my marriage was not your affair. Then I began to feel qualms. You seemed to set such a store on virginity and all that. And while I was wondering what to do, you suddenly sprang it on me that Dominic had been your greatest friend at Cambridge and you literally dragged him back into my life. I didn't know what to do, I was trapped. I'd finished with Dominic and I meant every word I said when I took those vows to you in the church. I thought it would all work out. But it didn't because Dominic wasn't as decent or as virtuous as you!"

Her eyes blazed at Sam. Her cheeks were fiercely red. She went on:

"He set out to wreck my life a second time—I admit it. But I didn't want him any more. I realised that I had only been infatuated with him and that it was you who meant absolutely everything to me. God knows, I've suffered. It's been absolutely hell for me. *You've* been happy, with nothing on your conscience ... Oh God! ..." she broke off, and burst into tears. "It must be wonderful to be so good. Well—I'm not. At least I wasn't, but if you want to go on punishing me for the past, okay—you can. I dare say I deserve it. Well, I'd better go away. You can divorce me for desertion and find a really good girl who won't let you down as I've done ..." Cressida broke off again, turned and rushed out of the room.

Sam stood motionless for a moment, staring after her. His face was distorted.

When he had first realised the situation between his wife and his old friend, he had been utterly shocked and bitterly hurt. He had gone on feeling like that until he knelt beside Dominic in the rain and watched him die; until he had heard those last words, gasped out with Dominic's final breath:

'Don't be a damn fool and hold it against poor Cress.'

Fatigue and shock had prevented him from sorting things out very clearly or sensibly during the drive back to Cowfold. Now after hearing what Cressida had to say, everything seemed so much more clear—the pieces were falling into place. As a whole, now it seemed obvious that he had expected too much. He might have had the right to expect it, but he had not allowed for the frailty of human nature. He had, in fact, behaved like a pompous prig. All those things Cressida had just hurled at him about being so virtuous, so lucky to have nothing on his conscience, hadn't made nice hearing. And they were true, but the last thing on earth he wanted was to *feel* virtuous. He had no right to condemn anyone. He had been stupid, perhaps, to place his Cressida on such a high pedestal. Poor darling, how she must have suffered, indeed. Gradually he was beginning to understand her predicament, her agony; she had tried to spare him instead of allowing herself to gain peace of mind out of a confession. She had thought of *him*. Not herself.

Old Dom was dead. Poor old Dom! He was finished with life and with the passions of man. But Cressida was very much alive. He couldn't accuse her of having been anything but a sweet and devoted wife since their marriage. *Of course*, he hated lies and deception. But suppose he had been in Cressida's position ... might he not have deceived her in order to preserve her happiness and belief in *him*?

Whatever Cressida and Dom had done, he, Sam, had behaved like a fool. He was just what Dom had told him not to be—a *damn fool*. If he lost his wife altogether, it wouldn't be so much because of Rome, but because of his own intolerance. Surely that was something he had thought about quite often and hated. A lack of tolerance. It was responsible for most of the religious persecutions and miseries in this world.

For a moment he continued to stand there, wrestling with his thoughts, while he lit a cigarette and smoked.

When he had finished his cigarette, he turned out the lights and went slowly upstairs. The door of the bedroom he shared with Cressida was shut. The door of the next room was open and showed him plainly his pyjamas and dressing gown laid out on the divan bed. Their 'spare'. It was not at the moment a very attractive room as it was still to be carpeted—there were only one small rug, a chest of drawers and a couple of chairs in here.

None of these things mattered, but what hit Sam between the eyes was the fact that Cressida had turned him out of their room and her bed. He had been banished.

He was so shocked already after the awfulness of Dominic's death and the events leading up to it, he was almost drained of emotion. But this action on Cressida's part revived his sensibilities. It seemed unkind and unwarranted. After all, he thought indignantly, he had not harmed *her*—she had hurt *him*—although, his tired mind argued, he had been reflecting downstairs that it was he who had been unkind. He had indulged in self-pity, which was unpardonable.

He opened the door of his and Cressida's own room. It was in darkness. The curtains were drawn back and the window wide open. He could not see his wife's face—just the little curled-up mound of her body under the bedclothes.

A great wave of tenderness, of love, replaced all that had lain in his heart before. He moved to the bedside, knelt down and pulled her gently into his arms.

"Oh, darling," he said brokenly, "oh, darling, *darling!*"

She had been crying. He could feel the wetness and heat of her flushed cheeks. But she responded instantly to his touch and his voice.

"Sam, darling Sam!" she sobbed his name.

He lay down on the outside of the bed and cradled her head against his shoulder. He covered her face with kisses, not ashamed of the fact that his own eyelids were stinging.

"Oh, Cressida, my darling . . . my love . . . I can't stand this. I couldn't bear the sight of that bed made up for me next door. It seemed like complete separation for us. It was murderous!"

"You showed me that you didn't love me any more."

"I didn't mean to, darling."

"But you *did*! You made it quite plain I've killed your love."

"You haven't—you couldn't!"

"But I have!" she gave another gasping sob. He could feel her shaking from head to foot. "I did you an awful wrong. I never should have married you letting you think that I . . ."

"Darling," he cut in. "I admit it was a shock, but do try and understand—I just wanted to sort things out. I needed time. You didn't expect me just to say quite casually: 'Oh so you lived with Dom in Rome, did you? How interesting!'"

He could feel her fingers beating against his back in protest.

"Of course not. *Don't* rub it in. I've had more than I can bear."

"Darling, that's how I felt until a few moments ago when I told myself that I had no right to be your judge. No right at all."

"You had," she moaned, "you had every right. To be cruel, too. Only I don't want to have to go on paying for the rest of my life for just that one ghastly mistake!"

He smoothed the hair back from her hot forehead.

"You shan't. I won't let you. I'll forget about it. Just give me time and I swear I'll forget it."

"You won't!" she moaned again. "You won't be able to, you'll always have it in your mind."

"You're quite wrong. When all this is over, I swear to God, I won't let the memory of Dom upset me for a single moment. I'm quite capable of putting it completely out of my memory.

You know I'm not the brooding sort. Oh, Cressida darling, do believe me. I swear I'll forget the whole thing absolutely—if you will, too."

She hugged him against her, still sobbing and shivering. Poor little thing, he thought, poor sweet Cressida . . . she was like a heartbroken child. Hot, damp, trembling. He had never felt a greater compassion for any human being. And apart from that he was conscious of immense relief. He was no longer separated from her. They were together again. Whatever had happened in the past, she was still his wife—his adored wife. Dom, poor devil, was dead. He couldn't come between them ever again.

"I do love you so much, Cress," he said, "I'd like to prove it to you. If you told me this moment that it was poor old Dom you really loved and that you'd only taken me on as second best, I'd forgive you. I'd even let you go—I wouldn't try to hold you—if that was the way you wanted it."

"No—*no!*" she almost screamed the words. Her fingers gripped him convulsively. "It's the very opposite. I nearly went mad when I thought you wanted to leave me. It was the end of the world for me. And I *didn't* marry you as second best. I'd loathe you to think such a thing. You became the first and best. I'd finished with Dominic. I fell in love with *you*. I tried again and again to make Dominic go away and leave me alone. He wouldn't," she added, her voice hoarse with emotion. "He just seemed to have the devil in him. He had no conscience. But mine's been nearly killing me, if you only knew!"

She felt his hand stroking her hair.

"My poor little thing—it must have been pretty good hell. All I can say is I'm sorry I was so blind, and didn't see how worried and upset you were."

"It was more than that. I couldn't bear the fact that I was sort of living a lie, every time Dominic came down here."

Sam gave a great sigh.

"Now, I understand why you didn't seem keen on him coming."

"Sam, it's all been too ghastly. I still can't ever make up to you for what I did in Rome. But please, please, let me try to be a marvellous wife to you now."

"You've been a marvellous wife all the time, darling. I was the happiest and proudest man in the world until the bombshell exploded, but I shall be again. You'll see!"

"Let's both make up to each other for all *this*," she said and groped for her handkerchief under her pillow and blew her nose violently; then tried to laugh. "Thank goodness it's dark and you can't see me. My face feels swollen to twice its size."

With a finger he traced the outline of the small nose, the fine cheekbones, the sweetly curved lips. He whispered: "It's the loveliest face in the world."

"You're so terribly nice to me, Sam."

He kissed her—a long kiss satisfying to them both.

"Darling, I'm getting cramp. I think I'd better take off my things and have a bath. Do you still want me to sleep next door?"

"No, *no!*"

When he came back to her, bathed and shaven, she had dabbed her own hot face with skin-tonic, brushed her hair and changed into a fresh, diaphanous nightgown. Her head ached—she had cried so much today. It had been such a terrible day, ending so terribly with Dominic's death. But peace seemed suddenly to be descending upon 'Dorians' again. Now that she was reconciled with her husband, she was fully conscious of the absolute sincerity of her feelings for him. She had never loved or respected him more. She had always known that he was a generous man, incapable of petty egotism. None the less, she felt humble in the face of his magnanimous treatment of her now and infinitely grateful for his love.

While they were lying in each other's arms, she said:

"I think it will be an awfully good idea if we neither of us talk about Dominic any more, but I *would* like to say tonight that I am terribly sorry you've lost your friend."

"That's sweet of you," said Sam, "It's all very sad, isn't it? He had such potentialities."

For a single instant, she, too, had a vivid memory of Dominic. Hard to believe that he was dead. And the '*Little Cat*' of his creation—that girl was dead, too. It was only Sam's wife who was very much alive, tonight.

14

ABOUT a year later, on a warm afternoon early in October, Lady Fennell sat at her desk in the small sitting room of her new flat in Holland Park, writing a letter to her son.

She had moved here about eight months ago.

She hated the lack of space after her big house. She hated the 'daily' who had replaced her staff of servants. She hated having no car. And she had almost begun to hate poor Coot who lived with her because life had seemed so incredibly dull since Guy (whom she still couldn't think of without resentment) had died leaving her so little.

But tonight, looking ethereal and beautiful in one of her old negligées and very much younger than her age, Franny was not so much filled with hate as with hope for the future. Life had suddenly changed. Things were moving. It was about these things that she was writing to Sam. She had wanted to phone him, but the wretched line to Cowfold was out of order. They were going on to some new system down there. Really, life in the country was so *primitive*, she reflected. She couldn't understand why Sam and Cressida didn't live in town. She wouldn't have thought that cold, uncomfortable house and garden worthwhile with poor Sam having to commute to London every day. However, he seemed to like it. And certainly she couldn't complain of the one week-end she had spent with them in August. Her daughter-in-law was becoming quite a good little cook and had made her very comfortable and welcome, and the pair of them seemed extremely happy. Franny had to admit that. They had gathered a nice circle of friends, and although money was short, and taxes and cost of living leaping up, the young couple seemed to manage very well.

Looking back, Franny thought what a shame it was that that clever, charming artist friend of Sam's—Dominic Miln—had been killed in a car crash last year. Dreadful thing! And so unnerving for poor Sam to have run straight into the wreck after visiting her in Hampstead that Sunday night.

Franny, pen poised in her exquisitely manicured hand, leaned forward and sniffed at a bunch of sugar pink flowers—hothouse roses on long slender stems. They stood on top of the bureau next to a newly-framed snapshot of a very good-looking young man on skis. A picture taken last February in Crans sur Sierre.

It was signed:

"For my adorable Franny from her Max."

It was about Max that Franny was writing to her son. She had meant to phone the news, but when they told her that the line might be out of order for at least another twenty-four hours, and this being Saturday she couldn't even phone Sam at the office, she thought she had better get down to a letter. Already she had covered four pages with her big, scrawly, loopy writing.

"No doubt you and darling Cress will be amazed to hear my news, but I hope you will be happy for me. I have been so lonely and miserable since Guy left us. I am sure you agree that I am not the type to live alone. So, darlings, I am going to be married again. Almost at once. As soon as I can get some clothes together and the final plans are settled.

You'll guess who it is, of course. Max von Brucka. I know you liked him when you met him at that dinner party I gave for him at the Mirabelle. Cress said how handsome he was. On the other hand, I know you don't care much for Germans. But what with our dear Queen's visit cementing the friendship of West Germany and England, so recently, I think it's time we stopped being unfriendly, don't you? Anyhow, Max is the son of an enormously wealthy father—head of the Brucka Steel Works. I shall be richer than I've ever been before with either of my other two husbands and I'm not ashamed to say that I like the idea. I just wasn't born to be poor, darling. I shall have a country house near Munich and a flat in Paris. Max is often in Paris on business and you know I ADORE that. And he's absolutely crazy about me. Of course, you're going to say I'm taking a great risk marrying a man younger than myself, but its only five years younger and Max says he's had lots of lovely girls in his life, but prefers older women. He adores sophistication. Please, darling, be angelic and don't let him know how old I really am. I'm afraid I've put your age as well as mine back about five years. But there's no harm in it—you'll be sweet about it, I am sure.

Max and I are being married at Caxton by special licence next week. We don't want anybody we know there. Even YOU. We're flying over to Paris directly after the wedding. Max has got a divine party laid on at the Crillon. Then we're going to our house in Munich where Max's mother has arranged a big party and I'm to be introduced to German society. They're all dying to meet me.

One good thing, I shall be able to send you children lovely presents and little cheques from time to time because Max is so fabulously rich, it isn't true. It really makes one wonder which of our two countries won the war when I first saw all the affluence in West Germany—that time I went over to meet his people.

I've told Coot she can keep this flat on, as she gave up hers to come and live with me and I'll pay the rent for her because she's a good old thing. But you and Cressida are to come and take all the silver and the good glass and china. It really belongs to you and I shan't need it.

I'm terribly happy so hope you will be happy for me.

Your still young and quite giddy
Franny"

Well pleased with herself, Franny read this scribble, put it in a large envelope and addressed it to Sam.

Then she got up and opened the door.

"Coot, darling, run my bath for me, will you?" she called to her companion.

What bliss it would be, she thought, to exchange Coot for her tall, fair, blue-eyed Max. He was angelic. And that divine income of his—it would be well worth saying good-bye to her title in order to become *Frau von Brucka*.

She glanced at herself in a mirror as she passed it. All the trials she had been through since poor Guy died had taken off some of her weight. She was as slim as a young girl; slimmer actually than Cressida, she thought. She must send the girl some of her nicest old suits and dresses when she bought the new trousseau which Max insisted upon paying for.

Max thought her figure perfect. He adored her silver gilt hair, cut like a page-boy's. He said she had the wickedest eyes and made young girls seem tame. He admired her wonderful taste. He was mad about her choice of clothes, too. He was going to buy her a sable jacket. That was something she had never had with either Sam's father or Guy. *Sables!* Oh, she thought blissfully, life was going to be marvellous. Max just couldn't *believe* that she was the mother of a boy as old as Sam (and she *had* taken off that five years). She always spoke to Max about 'the children' in Cowfold.

The telephone bell rang.

She sat on the edge of her bed and picked up the receiver. This was probably Max. He was taking her to a party at the German Embassy tonight. He would be coming to fetch her in his marvellous Mercedes Benz. What *luck* it was that her friends, Colin and Meryl Ryvingdon, had met him at that ski-hotel in Crans last February. They had introduced him to her when he came to London. Meryl now called him 'Franny's folly'. But Meryl was jealous, of course. No doubt *she* would like to have a young adoring golden-haired lover-boy like Max.

"Hello!" said Franny brightly into the phone.

"Hello," came Sam's voice, "It's me."

"Oh, hello, darling. I've just written you a *twemendous* letter," said Franny, using the lisp that she sometimes adopted when she wanted to show how gay she felt.

"You—writing letters? Gracious, what's come over you?" Sam asked.

"I've given you some *twemendous* news. By the way, I thought your line was out of order—that's why I didn't phone you."

"What's your news?"

"I don't think I'll tell you. I'll let you read my letter on Monday morning."

"Well, I've got some wonderful news for *you*. They put us

on the phone again about ten minutes ago and you're the first person we've rung."

There was silence. Franny felt suddenly a deadly presentiment.

"What about, darling?"

"Well, from our point of view, it's terrific, but I expect you'll feel we really owe you an apology, darling," came from Sam with a slightly bashful laugh. "We weren't certain until today when Cress saw a Brighton specialist. But now we know for sure. We're going to make you a grandmother."

Franny sat paralysed. She had gone quite white under her make-up. An awful sinking feeling replaced her excitement. She said:

"When?"

"Let me see—it should be about late May or early June. We're thrilled. So are Cress's family. Freda is absolutely beside herself."

"Of course," said Franny. Anger and even fear mounted in her at the thought of what she would be forced to tell Max. Of course, *Freda* would be beside herself!

"Franny, darling, don't be too upset. We do want you to feel happy about it."

"Oh, I do, I do!" said Franny in a hysterical voice.

"It only wanted this to make us absolutely happy," continued Sam. "Cress is terrifically well. I'd like a girl, but Cress says she wants a boy. If we do have a girl, we'll call her Frances after you."

Silence. Franny felt distinctly sick. Sam continued:

"What have you written to me about, darling?"

"You'll see," she said, gulping, "you'll see when you get my letter."

At this juncture, it appeared to Franny that her daughter-in-law had seized the telephone.

"Franny, isn't it *marvellous*? Aren't you pleased?"

"Delighted," said Franny thankful that neither of the 'children' could see her agonised expression.

"I want it to be a boy just like Sam—don't you think it would be terrific if I had a son as marvellous as yours?" continued Cressida, blissfully unaware of her mother-in-law's feelings.

"Terrific," Franny repeated the word like a machine.

Coot called from outside the door.

"Your bath's ready, dear."

Franny said good-bye to Cressida. She sat still, looking drawn and pinched. Not nearly as young as she had looked a few moments ago, she thought bitterly as she stared at her reflection in the mirror. Oh God, life—age—were catching up on her. She was going to be a grandmother. A grandmother. *Franny Fennell*. (Frau von Brucka.) And Max—a 'step-grandfather'. He'd *die*!

She knew that this was the age of glamorous grandmothers and that nobody really cared, but Sam's news, coming on top of the decision she had taken today to marry Max, seemed to her nothing short of disastrous.

Coot knocked, came into the room, and was horrified to find her friend in tears.

Down at 'Dorians', Cressida and Sam sat on the sofa together, drinking the aperitif they always enjoyed at this time after a Saturday's work in the garden. They were discussing the future of their child.

"I think it's going to be a very lucky baby," said Cressida.

"To have a mother like you, yes," said Sam. He admired his wife with her becoming summer tan and that slightly additional plumpness which, added to that beautiful maternal look in her eyes, seemed to lend her a new beauty. He really did adore his Cressida. And although they hadn't meant to have this baby quite so soon, they were both delighted.

They had been so happy all this year. The tragedy of Dominic Miln and all that had gone before, were things of the past; buried; forgotten. They had even agreed that the whole episode had in its way brought about a depth of understanding and love between them based on something much more concrete and honest than mere idealistic romance.

Cressida, herself, had never known such happiness. And today of course, was a red letter day. Following her visit to the doctor and his confirmation of her pregnancy, she and Sam celebrated with a drink at the Bungalow. Mummy, of course, was ecstatic. Dear old Daddy had offered to hire himself out any time as a baby-sitter, when the time came.

"Isn't it wonderful!" Freda had exclaimed. "A grandchild for us and for Uncle Simon a nephew—or niece. No—I feel it will be a boy."

"So do I and it's what I want," Cressida had said with a glance at Sam.

Now sitting alone with Sam, she discussed the baby as though it could be nothing *but* a boy. Sam, anyhow, was fast losing interest in his mythical daughter.

"Of course, he must go to my school, then to Cambridge," he said.

Then and then only, the shadow of Dominic fell across the brightness of the moment. They were both silent and suddenly sad.

But Sam reached for Cressida's hand and drew it against his lips.

"He'll be a lucky chap with such an alluring young mother to introduce to his friends."

"I rather envy him having such nice grandparents, I hardly remember mine," said Cressida.

"Well, I'm sorry he won't have a grandfather on my side or even a step-grandfather now poor old Guy's gone," said Sam.

"Do you think Franny was shattered by the news?" asked Cressida.

"I think she sounded a little shaken," smiled Sam. "She said she'd written me a long letter. I wonder what it's about?"

They knew—when that letter reached them on Monday.